The

December Rains

Jackie Clark

Wendilou Publishing

Any people depicted in stock imagery provided by Dreamstime.com are models, and such images are being used for illustrative purposes only.

Published by: Wendiilou Publishing
Wendy Brown

Cover design: Wendy Brown and Jackie Clark
Author photo credit: Jayde Lee Photography, Blayney

For more copies, contact the publisher c/-
212 Glenburnie Rd
Rob Roy NSW 2360
wendiiloupublishing@gmail.com
0468 998 268

Please note: This book has been written and published in Australia, and as such, Australian spelling conventions have been used throughout.

Dedication

To my most beautiful friend Brooke, for you on your 40th birthday.

Thank you for always being the one to give me a pat on the back, or a slap in the face. Life isn't life without you.

I love you so much Brookie.

Happy 40th Birthday my beautiful best friend.

The December Rains

Chapter 1

Misty rain hovered, almost weightless, in the air above the ocean. The clouds hung low over Regal Bay, dark and grey, like they would fall into the ocean at any moment. Tasting the salty sting in the air, Brooke ran slowly along the water line. Her brown and white Pit Bull terrier, an adopted shelter dog named Gambit, ran happily along beside her. Every step flicked dark sandy water up onto the back of her legs. Nearing the end of the beach she could see her car. It felt as though she was the only one in the world, not even a bird, just her and Gambit. She stopped, pushing her toe to the heel of her runners, she slid them off and walked down to the water's edge as Gambit watched from the sand. The water was cold, with each small wave lapping her feet, the sand pulled away from under them, making her feel like she was moving.

Brooke walked up the wooden steps, buried half in the sand, towards the carpark. She whistled sharply to Gambit, opened the car door, and with tail wagging, he jumped into his place on the passenger seat, slumping down onto his beloved tennis ball, hoping she didn't see him hiding it.

Brooke was 27, athletic, with long blonde hair. She was always, at heart, a nomad, a spontaneous, carefree person that moved around a lot. She'd had a simple childhood, growing up in the outer Sydney suburbs with her mother. She was the result of an affair which her mother had with a married man, although at the time, she didn't know he was married. Her mum told her the truth, never hiding it from her. Brooke was an independent girl who had an uncanny knack for fixing things and was incredibly close to her mum.

Her father, William, was the founder of Miller, Washington, and Associates, a prestigious law firm in Sydney. Her mother died when she was fifteen. She had moved in with her father and her half-sister Erin. With her mother gone she had nowhere else to go and to her father's disgust he agreed to let her live with him. Brooke never got along well with her father, he was strict and saw her as a problem he couldn't get rid of.

Growing up, she knew she didn't want to live out her father's grand plan of one of his daughters taking over the firm. She didn't want to be a lawyer; she didn't want a chaotic life. She always saw herself owning a café or restaurant and living a quiet life with lots of animals, she hated the city. Brooke was good at school and finished year 12 as Dux and went on to complete a degree in business management at the University of Sydney, working as a barista a local coffee shop on the weekends. None of her life's aspirations impressed him, leaving her to dream about the day she would be old enough to be free.

After selling the Mercedes her father gave her for graduating uni, a rebellious punch to the dominating city life for sure or maybe just her strict father, she bought an old Hilux ute and set out to find herself, to find somewhere that felt like home. As she always said to Erin, "It will speak to me, that's how I will know it's right".

She cruised her old Hilux ute down the dirt road beside the beach, through the dunes, back onto the main road to town, with music pumping loudly, bopping along while Gambit snoozed on the front seat.

Her life at Regal Bay had been quiet. She had made good friends with Fred Benson, the Owner of the only pub in town, who let her stay in one of the rooms upstairs, for free, in exchange for a few shifts at the pub each week. Regal Bay was a quiet beach-side community, more a passing-through town for travellers heading up the coast.

She had spent the last few months thinking about where to go from here, the time had come for her to move on. Late one night, after finishing a bottle of Red, a real estate ad on Facebook Marketplace caught her attention.

FOR SALE, deceased estate, The Blue Bell Café, a quaint little café for sale in the small town of Emery Creek. According to google, Emery was an old, rural, gold rush town with a population of five thousand people. The old timers cleared out much of the gold deposits a hundred years ago, but it still sometimes saw keen prospectors turn up, hoping to find the mother lode. It is in Central Queensland, far from the lush, beach village she had called home for the past year. The listing said it needed some TLC, perfect for someone looking for a tree change while starting their own business. The add said it included a furnished but small flat at the back of the café with lovely green grassed courtyard.

From the pictures she felt inspired. Typical of her quirky, spur of the moment nature. Over the next week, the café was all she could think about. She contacted the agent and found out there would be an auction the following

Saturday. What would the chances be that she could be lucky enough to buy it.

Brooke phoned into the auction with the agent. There was one other bidder against her, but they eventually pulled out and she listened to the final calls of the auctioneer and the hammer went down. It was hers. Brooke used the money she had saved from selling her Mercedes, signed the paperwork electronically, negotiated early settlement and permission to arrive at the property to make any changes to be ready to open her own cafe. She would pick up the keys from the real estate agent when she arrived in town. Her business management mindset screamed what a ridiculous idea it was, but she just couldn't put her finger on what it was about this little café that made her heart beat faster. It just spoke to her.

A few weeks later, Brooke said goodbye, kissing Fred on the cheek.

"Will you be ok, love?" he kindly asked her, extending his shaking hands to give her a hug. Fred was such a beautiful old man; he was always so kind to her and she was going to miss him.

"I'll be right." She pushed the last of the cheap, two-dollar-shop, striped bags of clothes into the back before pulling the cover across the ute tray, tightly pulling the elastic loop on the edge of the cover over the hook.

Early the next morning, before the sun rose, and without looking back, Brooke headed out of Regal Bay for the last time. She followed the Victorian coast for a while before taking the Ranges Highway heading towards the centre of

Australia. The drive to Emery she estimated, with the help of Google Maps of course, would take her 19 hours. She pulled over every few hours to stretch her legs and give Gambit a chance to run around.

Late in the afternoon, Brooke turned into the caravan park in Deckland, a small town near the New South Wales and Queensland border, for the night. The owner of the park was a lovely elderly lady who made an instant friendship with Gambit. She parked the ute alongside her cabin and carried in a small bag of things she would need, then walked the dog down to the river. Gambit ran down the bank and launched himself into the water to retrieve the ball she had thrown. She sat quietly on a tree trunk watching her boy swim and sniff around. Looking through the photos the real estate agent had sent her, a sudden angst came across her face, a prickle of goosebumps fluttered up her arms as the caller ID, Erin, came across her phone. She pressed the green circle. Despite spending most of their lives living with their mothers, the girls had become closer since being with their dad. They only had each other most of the time due to him having such a busy career. Even though they spent so much time together, Erin was the opposite to her. Erin loved the city, was slightly up herself, which suited the fact she was a lawyer. At least their father got one of them into the family business, she thought.

"Hey, Ez", Brooke said warmly.

Erin had always been dad's favourite and taken a position at the firm. Erin, with a break in her court schedule, promised her she would come and help her get the café started despite her disgust at having to travel into the bush.

"Do you know where this place is? The average temperature is 35 degrees, Brooke, I might die out there". Brooke rolled her eyes. Erin was always so dramatic.

"I'm sure you will be fine," Brooke laughed.

"It's not even funny, Brooke, I'll see you in a few days," Erin dictated down the phone.

Gambit walked up the bank and shook hard, sending water droplets all over her. Mouth wide open with shock, she sighed, and smiled at his happy little face.

"Come on, Gam, we have a big drive tomorrow."

Brooke was up before the sun again the next morning. She placed the cabin key in the after-hours box at reception and drove off into the dark. The sun crept slowly through the trees a few hours later to reveal the dry, red soil and a road that never seemed to turn. Only straight. By lunch time her ute was starting to struggle. It was chugging along until, finally, she pulled over. Opening her door, the heat in the air hit her in the face like concrete.

She unhitched and heaved the bonnet up. Brooke waited a few minutes for the steam to drift away before looking at the engine. She rested her elbow on the bull bar, hand supporting her chin. She was fooling herself if she thought she was going to find any problems, she had no idea what she was looking at. She checked her phone, no signal.

"Seriously?" With a heavy grunt, she pushed herself from the bull bar, turned sharply, and kicked a rock into the bush. Gambit was laying in the shade under a tree watching her intently.

"Don't look at me like that." She put her hands on her hips, and stood there for a few minutes, not saying a word, until the lump in her throat began to build. Trying to will away the imminent tears, she opened the driver's door and took out the blue Esky water cooler. The kind that had a cup built into the lid. She sat down with a hard grunt in the shade next to Gambit and took a long drink of ice-cold water, putting the cup down and pouring him some too.

It was half an hour later when she heard a rumble in the distance. It looked like a truck. As it got closer, she stood in the middle of the road and waved her arms around. The breaks from the road train loaded with cattle made a high-pitched squeal as it came to a stop. She watched the driver's side door open, and a yellow pair of work boots come, one at a time, down the rungs on the side of the truck.

The man was tall, had brown hair, and wore cargo type shorts and a tight black t-shirt which showed his muscular arms well. He had his sleeves rolled up neatly, and she could see a star tattoo on his forearm.

"Do you need help?" the man said, as he shut the door of the cab and walked towards her.

"Yes, my car is…. well, it's…. I am not sure what it is doing." Brooke laughed nervously.

The man looked unimpressed as he adjusted his baseball cap and walked over to her ute, the bonnet still up. She crossed her arms and followed behind him, watching as he looked intently into the engine bay.

"It was driving fine, and it just started struggling, a heap of steam came out when I opened the bonnet, if that helps." Instantly, she felt like a complete idiot as one of the cows in the back of the truck gave off a loud moo, probably laughing at her.

"For a start, you're low on water", he said, as Gambit sniffed around his feet, before looking up at her and raising an eyebrow.

"And oil, your fan belt is a bit loose too. When was the last time you had a service?"

Brooke thought about that for a minute and regretted opening her mouth as soon as the words came out.

"I have not had it serviced since I bought it."

The man walked back to the truck and came back with a large container of water and unscrewed the cap.

"I'm Brooke, by the way," she held out her hand as she introduced herself.

He gave her a cranky, side glance as he started pouring the water in. No hand shake. She raised her eyebrows and crossed her arms again. He half emptied the container into her engine and pointed towards the driver's door.

"Give it a try." He replaced the cap and walked back to his truck. She silently prayed as she turned the key, it took a few tries but finally she got it started.

"Where are you headed?", he asked her, slamming the toolbox down that was connected to the side of the truck. He didn't even look at her, he just looked into the back of the trailer through the side rails checking the cattle.

"Um, err, Emery," Brooke proudly exclaimed after a brief senior's moment of forgetfulness. He wiped the sweat off his forehead watching her childishly fumble with her words.

"You should get there easy enough if you don't push it too hard. If you plan to drive round out here often, you should probably get yourself a Cb radio, mobile phones are useless unless you're in town," he added, seeing her holding her phone.

She didn't have time to thank him, before he even finished his sentence, he was half-way into the cab of his truck. He just rolled his eyes and slowly started driving away.

"What a dumb arse," she said to Gambit as she judged his cold and unfriendly demeanour.

Brooke glanced at the clock on the dash. It was 2.52pm as she passed the sign saying Welcome to Emery. The vision she had in her mind of this moment was far from its sudden reality. The town had a wide main street with old, gold-rush style, single shop fronts with awnings over the path on each side. It reminded her of a town from an old western movie with dirt lane ways down between each of the shops. Despite the olden-day feel, there were quite a few people around, they looked to be mostly farmers and the only pub was on the corner near the roundabout, she read the name out loud to Gambit.

"The Roundabout Hotel, who would have guessed that, Gam?"

There was a central island down the far end of the street which carried through into the distance to a park with a wooden play-fort and slide. Regal Bay was so luscious, in comparison, besides the park here, there was no green grass, no beautiful trees or decorative features to the town. It was so hot, the skin felt like it was cracking off her face. It was dry, dusty, and everything seemed to be a shade of brown.

Brooke found the only yellow building, a few shops up from the pub as the email she received instructed, it had a tiny sign: Peter Archor Real Estate, on the front. She left the car running with Gambit in the passenger seat in the air conditioning.

Standing up straight and fixing her hair, she put on a confident smile and pushed the door open. A face looked up from the desk, the boy was young and looked like he was doing his homework.

"Can I help you?", he said politely.

Brooke smiled and introduced herself.

"Oh, my dad said you would be coming today. I'm Oliver, but most people call me Ollie," he shook her hand and rummaged through a pile of paperwork to find a yellow folder.

"I am supposed to be picking up the keys to The Blue Bell Café." She smiled.

He handed her the folder and a zip lock plastic bag full of keys. Brooke looked at the bag carefully. She guessed there to be at least 15 different keys, old, new, big, and small.

"My dad is on a call, I'm sorry, I work here after school for pocket money. I'll just ask him what he wants me to do, one moment." Ollie seemed like a nice young man. He quietly tip-toed into his dad's office before coming back not long after. "He said you're fine to have the keys, he will drop by tomorrow with the settlement paperwork".

"Oh that's ok, thanks Ollie," Brooke smiled.

"I don't suppose you can give me directions to the café?", she awkwardly asked the boy. Oliver looked so proud to be asked for his assistance. He walked her out the front of the shop and gave her very direct instructions.

"You drive towards the park, turn left at the coloured rocks, and then you can't miss it." He smiled and waved to her as she walked slowly back to her car. Gambit seemed like he was almost smiling at her as she got back in the air conditioning. Did he know something she didn't?

"I have a feeling I am going to regret this, Gam".

Chapter 2

Oliver's directions proved to be on point. She drove towards the park until she saw a collection of painted rocks. They were all different colours, were each the size of basket balls and were part of a decorative wall outside the playground. She turned left, and almost instantly, Oliver's instructions, once again, were incredibly correct. You couldn't miss it that's for sure!

Brooke pulled to the side of the road and just stared. The Blue Bell café was blue. Not a light, understated, blue but, in the only words she could think of to describe it, she blurted out.

"It's fucking blue!"

After sitting there in shock for a while, she continued, and pulled her ute into the small carpark in front of the café. She got out slowly, Gambit darted across and out the driver's side door after her. The café seemed a far more violent shade up close. All the walls, windows, ahh......everything was fucking blue.

The veranda was empty, there was two giant, you guessed it, blue pots on each side of the blue double doors. She looked at the bag of keys.

"What are the chances, Gam, the blue key would be for the blue door, of the blue café." She let out a whining, strangled laugh. Gambit waited impatiently as she slid the key into the door.

"Would never have thunk it," she mumbled to herself as the key turned and with a shove, she pushed the door open. A string dangling near the front door, she realised, controlled the lights, just like in her grandmother's old house in Sydney. Brooke tugged on it and with a click they, flickered a few times then the entire room lit up.

The inside was nearly as terrifying as the outside. Torn blue and white check curtains on the front windows screamed at her, tables and chairs were stacked high up the walls on the left side of the room. A central, of course, blue service counter caught her eye, more because of the bluebells that were painted evenly along the front. Behind the counter was another floor to ceiling grand statement of blue. Teacups, bowls, and glasses were stacked on the shelves, she thought twice about touching them due to the spiderwebs and years of layered dust caked heavily along the surface.

Brooke stood for a moment in silence. Her hands were shaking as she knelt very slowly on the floor and burst into tears while laughing at the same time. Gambit rushed over to her, licking her face, then forcing himself onto her lap in comfort before excitedly running off to explore again.

Brooke had been sitting there for a few minutes when a knock came at the door. She stood up quickly, wiped her face, and turned to find an old man standing in the doorway behind her.

"Good evenin', Bonnie Lass", he proclaimed in a distinct Scottish accent, shaking her hand.

"Hi," She smiled at him affectionately. It was very obvious that the charming elderly man was from Scotland. He wore a green and white tartan kilt, knee high socks, but in true Australian form, he had a truckie style singlet and crocs on his feet. He was short and portley, but his eccentric, jolly personality made up for his lack of centimetres.

"Me name's Colin, I live above the barber shop, aye, you must be Brooke, the new owner."

Brooke smiled, trying not to look like she had just had a moment on the floor, but on the other hand completely intrigued by his accent.

"It's nice to meet you, Colin, I am indeed Brooke, and my dog, Gambit, is around somewhere, I just got into town," she replied.

"How do ye like it?" He asked her, looking around, pointing around the room as she tried to interpret what exactly it was that he was saying.

"Oh, how do I like the place? Well, it certainly wasn't what I expected that's for sure".

"Ahhh, old Mrs Crawford certainly loved the colour blue, I suspect you will fix all that wee nonsense though", it was uncanny how much his accent gave her comfort, he sounded like Gerard Butler, but after a few pints.

"The place has been empty since she passed, going on 4 years ago. Aye, if ye need anything, don't be shy, Lass, just wanted to pop me wee head in and say Hallo" Colin said.

She nodded in thanks as he bowed his head to her and slowly shuffled out the door.

Brooke felt a bit better. Trying to escape the overpowering presence of blue, she continued on. Walking through into the kitchen, she was relieved to see nothing was blue. The kitchen looked well maintained and modern. There was a small walk-in cool room on the left beside two large fridges. The central island workbench was stainless steel and under it, on open shelves, was a variety of pots and pans.

"That's not so bad I guess, Gam," she stated to the dog as he waited for her to open the back door. Opening it and walking along a narrow path, she came to a tall, brown, rounded top, timber gate which, going by the pictures she had seen, led into, what she hoped was, her green grassy courtyard. Brooke took a deep breath and reaching through the hole in the gate to find the latch, opened it.

Even with the sun going down she could see the courtyard was huge, thankfully, it was green but overgrown. Gambit disappeared amongst the long grass as he sniffed around, it was secure, and Gambit would be safe here, which was a relief. There was a white, lace-like wrought iron table and chairs buried in the tall grass, broken, wooden flower beds along the longer side with a smooth stone path up the middle to the residence. Standing with the screen door open, Brooke shuffled through the bag of keys. Finally, one fit and the lock turned easily.

Brooke ran her hand down the wall till she felt a light switch. The front door opened onto a shared lounge and dining room with a small kitchen at the back. The furniture was typical of an elderly person, floral print, single lounge chairs and a heavy wooden dining table with brown and green suede covered, padded chairs. The kitchen had dark wooden cupboard door panels and a lime green laminate bench top, which would have surely been the rage in 1975.

There was a musty smell that lingered in the air, it was an old lady like smell, deep heat with a touch of red door perfume. She would need to give her flat a makeover as well as the café. Opening one cupboard after another looking for cups, she found a cupboard completely full of old Tupperware containers. She also found a blue willow dinner set, the Asian inspired kind that she often saw in antique stores in the city.

"The blue just never ends", she thought to herself.

There was a food gift hamper on the bench with a welcome note from the real estate agent. Brooke felt completely overwhelmed. What had she done? Was it too late to change her mind?

She opened her laptop and browsed through Temple and Webster's website; she desperately needed some new, fresh, modern furniture to shake off the funk that began to settle over her.

After eating a muffin from the hamper and getting Gam settled onto his bed for the night, she slid herself into the sleeping bag she had brought, in the main bedroom, where an old white and gold vintage bed just made her feel even more desperate to close her eyes and sleep. She scrunched up her pillow and closed her eyes, hopefully some inspiration would come to her overnight.

Brooke woke early. The unfamiliar noises would take a while to get used to. She made herself a cup of tea, again from the hamper supplies left on the bench, and sat at a table in the main room of the café with a notepad. It wasn't all bad, really, was it? There were positives. She glanced around the room in dire need to find a few.

The first and most important thing was a makeover. I'm sure old Mrs Crawford appreciated the blue, but Brooke felt like she was drowning in it. The tables and chairs were all in good condition, and from what she saw in the kitchen, there wasn't much to do in there. The main problems seemed to be cosmetic and nothing a few tins of paint wouldn't fix.

The café was in an old heritage style building and the folder given by the real estate said it was once a general store back in gold rush days. There was pressed tin on the ceiling and beautiful wooden boards on the floors. They were recycled and mismatched, had a variety of colours and grains, but in a unique way looked really good. The list was getting longer by the minute, she was an avid DIY'er and was determined to be involved with every aspect of the renovation and also try and do some of the work herself. Using her phone, Brooke, ordered some groceries, arranged a technician to connect the internet, and emailed a few gardeners for quotes to clean up the courtyard and the front of the café, she was feeling quite accomplished for it being so early in the morning.

Brooke drove into town and found the hardware store. Burrell's Hardware and Trade, the sign read in big bold red letters. She pushed the trolley through the aisles and before long she had filled up three of them. She browsed through hundreds of colours in the paint section before deciding on Vivid White and Forge Grey.

"Can I help you?", a voice broke through her concentration, and she let out a startled gasp.

"Oh, sorry, I was lost in my own thoughts, can I please have one can of white and two cans of the grey?", she asked, as she slid the colour swatches across the counter.

"You must be Brooke, I'm Leanne", the lady reached forward to take the cards.

"haha, yes, it seems everyone knows who I am", Brooke laughed.

"It's a small town, The Blue Bell has been empty for so long, Peter Archor comes in here all the time, he let us know that it had finally been sold"

Brooke raised an eye brow, she grew up in the city where no one knew nor cared about who you were, people in small towns know everything about everyone, it was going to take a while to get used to.

"Is there a lawn maintenance man in town you can suggest? I emailed a few this morning".

"Oh, I can assure you, no one here checks their email", Leanne laughed. "My brother owns a handyman business in town, I can have him call over to the Blue Bell and have a chat about what you want." Leanne shuffled through a selection of business cards on the bench, passing her the card.

Carter Anderson, Transport and Maintenance, it read.

"I can come help you paint if you want the company." Leanne offered.

"Oh, thank you, sure, that would be nice, I've got a few more things to do today, but if you're free to pop over in the morning, that would be nice." Brooke, with the help of Leanne, loaded her three trolley loads into the back of her ute.

"I'll catch you in the morning then, I'll bring some coffee," Leanne proudly said, waving as Brooke drove off.

Chapter 3

Brooke spread plastic drop sheets all over the floor and put together the paint rollers. Leanne arrived as promised with 2 extra-large cups of coffee. Taking a sip, Brooke's left eye twitched a little as she swallowed it. Not the best coffee she had ever had, that was for sure.

"So, I'm thinking the forge grey for the walls and white for the skirting boards and sills," Brooke said, holding the colour swatch up against the wall.

"I really like it; old Mrs Crawford would be beside herself to see the blue covered up".

Brooke smiled, dipped the roller into the undercoat and pushed it up the wall. It felt amazing to see the blue slowly disappear. It felt so suffocating.

"What's the go with her anyway?" Brooke asked Leanne.

Leanne dipped her brush into the white and proceeded to deliver the best version of the story in town.

"Well, Mrs Crawford was born and raised in Emery, her husband immigrated to Australia and they both lived in Emery for over 70 years. Her husband bought her the Blue Bell as a gift for their 30th wedding anniversary. She was, as you would have realised by now, a big lover of the colour blue." Leanne finished the window sill and dipped her brush back into the can.

"Old Mr Crawford was fishing in his boat one day down at the river bout 10 years ago, near the park actually. A storm sent a heap of debris down the river. No one knows exactly what happened, his boat nor body were ever recovered, they found a heap of his belongings though. Was a big story back when it happened, my grandfather always used to tell stories and that was one of them. Mrs Crawford continued to run the café on her own until she also died, about 4 years ago now. They had a son but I'm not sure what happened to him, the bank put it up for sale after she died". Leanne wiped the sweat from her brow as she dipped her brush again into the paint can.

"Why has no one ever thought to buy it?" Brooke asked.

"A few people say its haunted, others say its because the place needs so much work".

"Haunted hey, I suspect that the only thing haunting this place is the colour". Brooke thought on that notion for a moment. Its not every day someone suggests that a place is haunted.

A few hours later, they had the first coat done when Brooke heard the noise of a car.

Leanne opened the door, standing there was the one and only Mr Dumb Arse.

"This is my brother, Carter," Leanne announced as he took off his baseball cap, tucking it under his arm. Brooke watched his yellow work boots step one at a time onto the plastic covered floor.

"We have met," Brooke said bluntly. Carter slightly laughed and smiled as he looked smugly up at the ceiling trying to not look directly at her. Carter wore nearly exactly the same outfit he had on the day he stopped on the road to help her. She didn't notice how nice his smile was, however, because, from what she remembered, he was too full of himself to smile that day.

"Since when?" Leanne demanded from her brother.

"This is the ignorant city girl I told you about the other day, who was stuck on the side of the road with no radio".

"Excuse me?" Brooke fumed.

Leanne laughed nervously hoping to diffuse the situation.

"Oh, well, not to worry, I'm sure we can make sure she gets one installed so it doesn't happen again," she said directing her comment at her brother.

"Lee said you wanted some help with the yard, I can do it this morning if you still need it done."

Carter was far from polite but none of the other people had returned her emails. She was starting to realise that this dumb arse with the dimples may be the only one she could get.

Brooke agreed and handed him the list she had made for him to do. Carter rolled his eyes and put his cap back on. One yellow work boot at a time, she watched him leave.

With Leanne's help, they had the inside painted by the end of the week. It was clean and fresh. The white and grey really looked amazing alongside the pressed tin ceiling and mismatched floorboards. Leanne helped her tile the front of the service counter with a lighter grey accent tile. Brooke had the outside sprayed by local painter, Walter Fitzgerald, it was a similar grey and white accents. The café had become the *it* place to be, so many locals had stopped by for a snoop to meet the new owner and news soon spread around town that the grand reopening would happen the following week.

Brooke sat with Colin on the bench in the park across from the café, and watched the new sign go up above the awning at the front. In beautiful script lettering, Brooke's Place.

"Aye, Lass, she looks mighty fine." His legs stretched out in the sunshine as he admired the new sign.

Deliveries had been arriving all week, with new plates and kitchenware, and a variety of other bits and pieces she had on her list. The biggest prize of all was a beautiful Silver Chef Coffee Machine. Now life was complete. Finally, decent coffee.

Carter had finished the lawns, replanted the front pot plants in beautiful new grey pots and built the fence around the front carpark. He watched Brooke through the front window as he replanted the front garden, Gambit was sun baking on a wooden bench against the wall, his foot flicking into the air every now and then, dreaming. She glanced up at him, instantly cutting the stare.

Brooke unwrapped the new cups, placing them in the space at the top of the coffee machine. Her blonde hair was pulled back into a ponytail leaving little wispy bits around her face that formed ringlets. She had a glow about her that was hypnotising. He shook it off, tipping the last of the potting mix from the bag.

It was coming together nicely. Peter Archor came by to have Brooke sign the final documents for the sale.

"It looks amazing, even the air conditioning is now working", he exclaimed as he looked around the room. "Like, I really can't believe it, Mrs Crawford, I think, would be impressed even though the blue is gone".

"Would you like to be the first person in town for a fresh coffee, Peter?"

He smiled eagerly sitting on the stool at the counter. She tamped down the freshly ground coffee until it was smoothly and perfectly flat. She pushed the button and the hot water began to flow through, the fresh coffee dribbled down into the cup. The smell filling the air was delicious, she steamed the milk before tapping the bottom of the silver jug on the counter. Holding the cup on a gentle angle she poured the milk in, leaving a perfect fern pattern on the top, placed it on the saucer, and slid it across the counter to Peter.

His eyebrows peaked high as he sipped, leaving a frothy patch on his top lip. He didn't speak, he just made a relaxed hum and closed his eyes.

Brooke smiled as the door flung open with a loud crash hitting the wall behind. In the doorway stood a tall, tanned, brunette woman in heels, a pencil skirt and stripped shirt that tied in a bow at the front of her neck, she looked very professional.

"What the hell have you done?", she said rudely as she looked around the room, far from impressed.

Brooke recovered from the shock and ran across the room excitedly. It was her sister, Erin, she looked like she didn't belong in a small dusty town like Emery, that's for sure.

"Peter, this is my sister, Erin".

Peter, still with his mouth slightly open in shock, stood from his stool and walked timidly over for the introduction then excused himself and left quickly.

"Coffee?"

Erin laughed.

"Of course, do you have anything stronger for later though, I'm gonna need it." Using a napkin, she brushed the stool off before sitting down.

"What were you thinking, how are you going to make a living in a hole like this?".

"Lucky you were not here last week, you would have had a lot more to say then, I assure you", she laughed and tapped the jug again and gently poured the milk leaving a perfect layer of foam on top.

"I hope you're planning to stay for the opening, you do remember how to make coffee don't you?"

"It's probably the only thing from my uni days I want to remember," Erin mumbled as she took a sip.

"You didn't tell Dad did you?" Brooke asked her seriously.

"What? That you sold the car he bought you to buy a dilapidated café in the middle of woop woop." Erin snapped, as she pulled out her laptop and set it up on the counter. Erin was in every way a city girl, she worked constantly and was very good at her job.

Brooke wiped down the steam handle on the coffee machine.

"Come to think of it, when you put it that way, I'd probably prefer you didn't say anything".

Over the next few days, Erin created a website and social media pages for Brooke's Place, she called in a few favours with suppliers in Sydney for coffee beans and ordered custom printed bags and boxes to use for takeaway orders. All the small personal touches made a big difference. Brooke let Erin take the reins when it came to marketing, it gave her something to do and, frankly, stopped her complaining about everything. Erin and Brooke visited the local newspaper to place an add for the café's grand reopening the following Monday.

Erin arranged high profile Sydney coffee expert, Alexander Koh, to be there on opening day as a special guest.

"You do realise that no one here will know who he is, don't you?" Brooke laughed.

"It doesn't matter, I know who he is, this town needs a touch of class, something it severely lacks, I'm afraid".

"Hang on, before we go, I just want to call in and chat to Ollie". Brooke left Erin standing out on the footpath, rolling her eyes, and tapping her pointy heel on the ground while she went into the real estate. A few moments later she came back out with a smirk on her face.

"I just gave Ollie a job". Brooke looked really pleased with herself.

"The kid is like 8". Erin accused.

"He is 14, actually, and a really nice boy".

Brooke sat on the veranda of the café sipping a glass of red wine with Gambit rolling in the freshly cut grass beside the carpark, giving his white patches a light tinge of green. The sun set projected a deep orange glow across the sky. The cooler air started to settle in as the sun went down, taking the toasty sting out of the air.

Carter closed the side gate as he carried the last of his tools back to his ute, Gambit had quite the liking for Carter and leapt up into the back of his ute hoping to go for a ride.

"Not today, buddy". He smiled as he lifted him back down. He opened the driver's side door and went to step in.

"Thank you for your help today". She called out. Carter smiled and closed the door. He reversed back down the carpark to where she was sitting, Erin joining her with a towel wrapped around her wet hair.

"I'll be in on Monday, to sample the coffee". He smiled.

One thing she noticed was the way his eyes kind of squinted as he smiled. There was something about Mr Dumb Arse that gave her goosebumps. That smile was cheeky but gentle. She watched him drive away. Erin stared at her across the table and cleared her throat loudly.

"What?" Brooke tried to look innocent.

Chapter 4

The Grand opening of the café came around quickly, and Mother Nature played nice with a cooler day. The veranda at the front of the café had beautifully set tables for guests to eat outside. Inside was perfectly styled, tables dotted around the main room with Erin's custom-made menu cards in the centre, nestled neatly between the salt and pepper. The once blue wall behind the counter was now grey with Brooke's Place in large, beautiful, white lettering just like the front signage, there were lights on each side of the script lettering, shaped like giant light bulbs, hanging simply on black cords from the ceiling over a long, polished timber bench with stools. There were beautiful tall indoor palms at each end. It was city simplicity with a country twist.

The centre counter had a glass unit on the left, it had shelves to display food items, and the coffee machine was on the right with the register, leaving the centre clear to serve people.

Dave Price was her chef. He and his wife, Stephanie, had moved to town recently from the city also, she was a doctor and had opened a new General Practice. Something the town desperately needed. Leanne had also moved from the hardware store to work as her waitress.

Dave had prepared a fresh modern breakfast and lunch menu for the café which was written on the back wall in white marker where customers could easily see it when ordering. He made a selection of slices and cakes available each day, as well as weekly specials.

Alexander Koh, the coffee extraordinaire Erin had organised, arrived shortly before open. He was from Japan, tall, with long dark hair and was wearing a suit. He didn't speak much English so was quiet but took in all that was around him. Unpacking several copies of his latest book, he moved a plant from the counter and leant his books neatly where it was sitting. He walked behind the counter, took his suit jacked off and handed it to Erin who promptly stood beside him at his beck and call.

Erin looked around one last time. "Well, I'll give myself credit, the place is perfectly presented". Alexander bowed his head in agreement.

The staff wore black shirts with the Brooke's Place logo on the back. Brooke glanced across the room to Leanne who smiled and nodded. She walked across the creaky, mismatched floorboards, and for the first time, turned the sign around on the door.

"We are open," she declared. She smiled as she glanced outside to see people waiting to come in.

Erin, Brooke, and Leanne excitedly served customer after customer. The place was packed. Peter Archor came in and was delighted to see his favourite pecan pie on one of the cake stands with a glass lid on the counter. Brooke cut him a slice. And he sat with his coffee and pie on a stool along the back wall. A beautiful big bunch of multicolour flowered arrived, delivered by Sam, the local florist. Brooke read the card. *Congratulations on Brooke's Place* regards, your friend, Fred. She placed them in a vase at the end of the counter.

"Aye, Brooke's Place", Colin read out loud the words on the back wall. "You have done a fine job, lass", he said as he looked through the glass at all the cakes.

"Would you like some scones? On the house, just for you, with jam and cream, of course", Brooke said smiling.

"That's mighty fine of you". Colin was standing at the counter in his usual kilt, socks, and crocs ensemble.

"I'll bring it over to you, take a seat".

Perfect round scones on a rectangle serving board with tiny side bowls of jam and whipped cream. Colin sat at the table in the far corner. The bell on the front door jingled as two policemen came in.

"Hey, you must be Brooke," the taller Constable asked.

"Appears everyone knows me, yes, I am Brooke", she shook both of their hands. The taller one was young and easy to talk to, he was happy to stand and chat while the other, shorter, Sergeant with Williams on his badge walked away quickly, sitting at a table on the veranda.

She read his name badge; Constable James McDonald.

"I'm James, my not so cheery colleague is Paul, can I grab 2 flat whites and I'll get a couple of the custard tarts you have in there", he said pointing through the glass on the counter.

"No worries, it won't be long".

Brooke took the board with Colin's scones over to his table.

"Enjoy, my friend". She said quietly as she placed the plate in front of him on the table, continuing to clear empty plates from the tables on the veranda when she caught a glimpse out of the corner of her eye of yellow work boots. Her skin prickled as she walked inside to see Carter standing at the counter ready to order. She handed Leanne the plates. She couldn't explain it, but suddenly she became clumsy and tongue tied. It wasn't like her at all. She was realising more than ever that this dumb arse instantly made her nervous.

"What, er, can I get you?"

Carter took off his hat and tucked it under his arm as he looked at the menu.

"Just a coffee, black, no sugar, might grab that chocolate brownie too", he said pointing to the biggest one through the glass. "I'll be at a stool in the back," he said as he tapped his card on the eftpos machine.

Alexander made his coffee. Brooke put the brownie that he pointed to on an eclectic square plate. She felt such a need to impress him, to make the presentation perfect, she sprinkled some icing sugar with a B stencil onto the top, placed a small fork alongside it, and walked over to him. He leant back on his stool, giving her room to lean past him and place the plate and his coffee. It felt like slow motion and the smell of his sweat mixed with his cologne imbedded in her nose.

"Thank you". It was almost a whisper as he glanced up to her face.

"You're welcome", she said. Catching herself in the moment, she smiled and walked out to the kitchen.

Dave was making the last of the lunch orders. Lunch was scheduled between 11.30 and 2pm.

Quiche, corn fritters, chicken Caesar wraps, and house meat pies served with mash, peas, and rich gravy. She pushed the order slip on the spike and took out the finished meals. She could feel the energy in the room almost hover like a silent insect hanging in the air. Her body tingled from head to toe, feeling Carters eyes gave her stomach an awkward, nervous burn. Brooke tried hard not to look at him, collecting finished cups and plates from the surrounding empty tables. She became so distracted at trying to ignore him that she bumped into him as he was leaving, spilling a half empty cup of coffee down the front of his shirt.

"I'm so, so sorry". Brooke gave him a serviette. Carter smiled at her fumbling nervously before she conceded, sighed, and stepped out of his way.

"You know how I take my coffee now; I'll be back tomorrow". He put his cap on and walked out the door with a cheeky smile.

Suddenly she noticed the table where Colin was sitting, his scones were still on the table exactly where she had left them, they were untouched, and Colin was gone.

Carrying the plate out to Dave she tipped the scraps into a bucket they had for food scraps that Ollie took home each afternoon for his chickens, he in exchange, shared his eggs with her.

"Did you see Colin leave?" She asked Erin who was standing at the counter passing Alexander a clean cloth to wipe the coffee machine.

"Who's Colin?"

Brooke pointed across the room at the table where he was sitting.

"He was sitting over there earlier, old man wearing a kilt, hard to miss".

"I can tell you right now I have not seen anyone wearing a kilt today and if I had I would have certainly remembered".

Alexander was packing his books back into his bag and put his jacket on. He still had not said a single word to Brooke the entire day. Leanne turned the sign around on the door at 2.30pm after the last table left. Dave, Leanne, and Brooke watched as Erin put the dockets on the counter.

"Breakfast we did 15 orders and lunch we did 22, which is pretty good considering its only day one, but the best part of the day, 417 coffees".

Brooke hugged Erin as everyone clapped. "By the way, I'm flying back to Sydney with Alexander this afternoon, it's too bloody hot here, its seriously drying out my skin". Erin huffed and went back to Brooke's flat to get her suitcase.

Out of the blue, Alexander reached out his hand to Brooke. She shook his hand before he handed her an autographed copy of his book. Looking down at the inscription it read; "Congratulations on your grand opening".

"Thank you for coming all this way, I can't thank you enough". Alexander bowed his head to her, and she acknowledged him by doing the same. Erin came back through the kitchen pulling her suitcase behind her. Her sunglasses sat on the tip of her nose.

"Well, my work here is done, don't go and wreck it now, will you". Erin, even though she came across as blunt and most definitely more than often, rude, meant well.

Brooke walked Erin and Alexander out to the carpark where a taxi waited to take them to the airport.

"Take care of yourself". Erin wasn't one for feelings.

"You too". Brooke kissed her on the cheek. Erin pushed her sunglasses back up her nose with her index finger and waved goodbye.

Brooke stood with Leanne on the veranda and watched the taxi drive away.

"Your sister is certainly a lot of work".

"Oh yeah", Brooke agreed.

"Hope your brother wasn't to upset about his shirt today, I'll buy him a new one if the stain doesn't come out".

Leanne tapped her on the shoulder, smiling, she sighed.

"You could have ripped a hole in it, and I don't think he would have cared".

Brooke walked along the river front not far from the café with Gambit. The water was calm and had a gentle flow. She threw his ball far into the water, Gambit launched himself into the water to retrieve it. She leant up against a tree and looked back on her little piece of paradise. She was really starting to like Emery. Everyone was so welcoming towards her the last few weeks. The first day exceeded her expectations. It felt good to look at how far she had come with Brooke's Place in just under a month. She felt proud of herself. Walking back towards the cafe Brooke noticed Colin walking through the park and yelled out to him. He didn't seem to hear her and soon walked out of sight. He sure was an interesting fellow.

Chapter 5

It was a beautiful Saturday morning. The toasty sting in the air seemed tame that morning. Oliver was waiting outside patiently with a basket of eggs.

Brooke smiled and let him in.

"Good morning, Ollie".

Pulled up in the carpark, well before open, was a black 4x4 and camping trailer. A few minutes after she turned the sign around to open, the couple came in.

"Can I help you?" Brooke asked.

The woman had beautiful long hair and wore a check patterned dress and white sandals. The man wore jeans and a maroon shirt, his beard was long and nearly reached his belly button, he wore a light-coloured cowboy hat.

"Yes, we would love to grab a table for breakfast, just a black tea for my husband, but first, I need the biggest cup of coffee you have". The woman sighed with a tired smile. Brooke laughed.

"Let me show you to a table, are you travelling?" Brooke led them across to one of the front tables near the windows.

"We are on the way home, been driving for 2 days. Can I just have poached eggs on toast, and he will have one of your big breakfasts also please," the woman said as she browsed the menu. "Oh, with extra bacon", she smiled.

"I'll be back in a moment with your coffee". Brooke took the order out to Dave in the kitchen and returned shortly after, placing the cups down on the table.

"Are you the owner?", the woman asked.

"Yes, I am Brooke".

"This is such a beautiful spot you have here, this is my husband, Stuart, and my name is Claire".

"Pleased to meet you, where are you headed?". Brooke asked.

"We have a property near Reffshore in Victoria, we have been up the top end on our honeymoon."

"Oh, that's fantastic! It would be beautiful up there. Well, breakfast won't be long, let me know if you need anything".

Olliver cleared plates from the tables and took orders out. He was loving working there and his face beamed with happiness which didn't go unnoticed by the customers. Several pointing out what a nice young man he was.

Brooke stood at the counter looking through a gardening magazine, she was completely engulfed in her own thoughts when she was interrupted by a man clearing his throat.

"Uhh hum".

Brooke looked up to see Carter. Hat, as usual, tucked neatly under his arm looking at her flicking through the magazine with an inquisitive smile.

"Building a garden?". He asked.

"Oh, um no, was just thinking about giving my courtyard a makeover, are you having your usual today?".

"That would be great thank you, you know I do know a really good gardening expert who would be able to help you, in exchange for perhaps a free coffee, or two". Carter gave her a cheeky smile that gave her goosebumps from head to toe.

"I see, well then I could probably arrange a few if he proves to do a good job". She made his coffee and pressed the lid down gently, sliding it over the counter to him. He reached to grab the cup, his fingers slightly touching hers.

"The café is closed tomorrow. If you want to let the expert know that I'll be ready about 9am to go through some ideas, that would be great".

Brooke smiled as Carter put his hat back on and seemed to skip out the door. She laughed to herself. Claire and Stuart stood up and collected their belongings, Brooke walked over and handed Claire another large coffee and a brown paper bag with a chocolate brownie inside.

"It's on the house, happy honeymoon".

"Thank you so much, breakfast was amazing. Compliments to the chef, they were the best poached eggs I've had in years".

Brooke walked Stuart and Claire out and waved goodbye when she saw Colin sitting on the bench in the park across the car park and waved. Colin smiled and nodded his head towards her.

"Thanks again", Claire yelled from the passenger window as they drove away. Brooke looked up again to see that Colin had gone.

"I guess I will chat to him another time". She thought to herself.

After lunch, Ollie turned the sign around on the door. She passed him an envelope with his first pay. Ollies eyes lit up like a Christmas tree. He opened it looking at the arrangement of notes inside.

"So many have sung your praises, I thought you deserved a bonus".

Ollie pranced happily to the kitchen to retrieve the chicken scrap bucket and let himself out. Brooke stood at the window looking at the clouds, it looked like a storm was building, lightning flashed off in the distance before a deep rumble was heard. She always had loved storms.

Chapter 6

Brooke woke early the next morning and sat in the courtyard with a coffee. Gambit was restless and barking more than he usually did.

"Gam, enough". She scolded.

A knock on the gate sent Gambit out of his mind. Jumping up and down like he had springs in his legs. Carter reached through the hole and lifted the latch, Gambit threw himself at his feet, rolling over for a belly rub.

"Aren't you a good boy". Carter rubbed his belly, Gambit jumped back up with his tail wagging furiously. "Think he likes me; he has good taste". Carter looked down at Gam as he sat leaning up against his leg.

"Ahhh, does he? I guess he has a sixth sense when it comes to people, unfortunately, he's not the greatest guard dog".

Brooke handed him the magazine with post it notes marking the pages with notes of things she liked. Carter looked through the pages, raising his eyebrows and chuckling to himself.

"Well, you have it all organised, I see". Carter took a measuring tape out of his pocket. He ran it along the longer side wall, then across the others. Roughly ten metres long and five metres wide. There was a tree at one end. Carter wrote some notes and took more measurements. He ran his hand up the trunk of the tree and picked a leaf, scrunched it up and lifted it to his nose. It had a similar scent to lemon leaves when you break them, releasing the light citrus smell.

"May be a coincidence but this tree I'm pretty sure is called a Blue Javelin".

"Of course, it is, fucking blue", she mumbled to herself.

Carter and Brooke went to the hardware store and then to Hatton Nursery and Garden Supplies to get some plants. Brooke's ideas were not bad, in fact, Carter was quite impressed by what she had in mind. He watched her walking around the endless rows of plants, reading the information tags on various shrubs that took her fancy. He couldn't deny the instant chemistry they had, tormenting and teasing each other. The friendly banter that, more times than not, was deliberate flirting. She loaded bags of dark brown bark chips onto the trolley and selected tall new pots to put on each side of the door.

Carter built new raised garden beds around the walls and installed a watering system that was connected to the water tank beside Brooke's flat. A vegetable garden on one end with silverbeet, zucchini and pumpkins, and flowers across the longer wall. Brooke used the pressure washer Carter bought with him to give the stone path a revamp, amazed at how removing the years of dirt and moss gave it a whole new fresh feel.

Carter watched Gambit sniffing around the base of the tree. He was sitting on the grass putting together another pipe and dripping head for the watering system. Brooke bought a jug of ice water out from the kitchen and sat it on the wrought iron table, pouring Carter a glass. Gambit started barking and pawing at the ground. Carter sprang onto his feet and leapt across the grass grabbing Gambit by the collar pulling him back with a loud yelp across the yard to where Brooke was sitting.

There was a Snake. Carter slowly walked towards where he saw it move last. He used the shovel and lifted the empty plastic pots and hose out of the way. He lent down and, fast as lightning, reached down and grabbed the tail of a Python. He held it up. The snake would have been at least 5 feet long.

"Oh my god", Brooke opened the screen door to her flat and put Gambit inside.

"Pass me that garbage bin?"

Brooke took the lid off, emptying the rubbish onto the ground, Carter lifted the bin in his free hand and lowered the snake down into it, Brooke jumped forward with a blood curdling scream, slamming the lid down on top of the bin still screaming. Carter laughed hard as he crouched beside her, both of them still holding the lid down. Brooke was wide eyed and breathing like she had just ran a marathon.

"It's just a Python, it won't hurt you". Still chuckling he grabbed her hand. "It's ok".

Brooke instantly had goosebumps up her arms as he touched her.

"I've never seen a snake before; well, I have at the zoo but not, um, in person".

Again, he watched her fumble with her words. It was strangely cute. She was having a panic attack; he just couldn't help himself and jerked suddenly over the bin towards her.

"Raaahhhh". He yelled.

She screamed again jumping up and down on the spot. She was far from impressed as she knelt back down beside him and started to cry from the shock.

"You're ok, I promise," he laughed. "I'm sorry".

He touched her cheek, wiping away a tear. She looked into his eyes. He felt bad. Without much thought he leant forward to kiss her, taking her mind instantly off the snake. She found herself kissing him back before she took hold of her emotions and pulled away. It wasn't a long kiss, but Brooke felt it in every inch of her body. Gambit barked loudly which startled her back to reality.

"I better let him out". She said wiping her face. "Um, would you like a glass of water?".

"Nah, I better get this fella off to somewhere he won't be any more trouble". Carter lifted the lid to check on the snake. Looking back at her, he latched the bin lid shut. He moved to stand right in front of her, lowered his head again and kissed her cheek without any hesitation. "Don't suppose you want to have dinner with me?". He asked her quietly as she looked up at him.

"Um, I'll think about it". Fumbling again with her words which only seemed to happen around him.

"I'll be in tomorrow".

"Oh, you will?" She questioned, as he started to walk away.

"For a coffee."

"Black, no sugar," she recited his coffee order to him.

Carter smiled, lifting the latch on the gate, Gambit whimpered through the holes in the gate as he left.

"Dumb Arse". She muttered to herself.

Chapter 7

Brooke opened the door to the café, smoky haze hung in the air. Looking across to the park and down the side street she couldn't help but feel like the town had been abandoned, it was an eerie feeling. Brooke saw Colin sitting on his usual bench at the edge of the park. Brooke walked across the carpark towards him as Dave arrived to start the breakfast prep.

"Good morning, Colin". She sat down beside him as Gambit sniffed around the trees.

"Not a nice day, aye Lass". He said looking around at the smoke.

"There must be a fire close by". Gambit ran back across the carpark and slumped down on the café veranda.

"Whatever is burning is in town". Colin pointed towards the main street. She saw a dark pillar of smoke high in the sky.

"Oh, I'll um catch you later, Colin" Brooke said. Colin waved as she hurried across the carpark to hear the café phone ringing.

"Hello, Brooke speaking".

It was Peter, the town Library was on fire.

"The firies have been here since 4 o'clock this morning".

Leanne walked in the door ready to start her shift.

"I'll get Dave to make some bacon and egg rolls and bring them down, if there is anything else they need let me know". Brooke hung up the phone.

"The library is on fire". Brooke gasped to Leanne.

"Yeah, I heard, Carter called me earlier, he is down there helping with the volunteer brigade, it looks like it may have spread into the pharmacy next door".

"Do you have any idea what started it?". Brooke asked as she packed bottles of orange juice into a box.

"Not sure, Carter didn't give me too many details".

Within the hour, Brooke loaded her car with a box of bacon and egg rolls wrapped in alfoil and another box with orange juice and fresh extra hot coffee neatly stacked in cup trays so they wouldn't spill. She drove carefully down the main street towards the library. There was a Police barricade in place. She pulled slowly in beside Constable McDonald.

"Hey, Brooke, sorry but I can't let you down there". James stood at the driver side window.

"I've bought down some breakfast and coffee for the Firies".

James peered in the window on the back to see the boxes laying neatly across the seat.

"Alright, you can go down, park out front of the supermarket, there is a tent set up there with the Ambo's, you can leave it there".

"Help yourself, Constable", she motioned to the back seat. He opened the back door and picked up a cup of coffee and a roll.

"Thanks, Brooke, you're a legend".

Brooke parked her Ute where he told her to. She opened the back door and carried the boxes one at a time to the Ambo tent. The scene was that out of a movie. The library was 50 metres from the tent, it was fully engulfed with several groups of firemen with fire hoses going at once to try and bring it under control. She could hear the creaking of the timber and metal roof as it struggled to stay up.

She could see Carter and several of other men desperately passing boxes out of a side door that led to an underground storage room in a relay line setting them down in the middle of the street. The pile had a least 40 document boxes and hundreds of books in random piles. One after another they passed the books down the line until a fireman yelled to them that they had run out of time. Carter, with his hands on his hips, looked up to the sky trying to suck in as much fresh air into his lungs as he could. A man signalled from the Pharmacy end and a call came across the radios. She could hear them talking to each other. The Pharmacy was under control. They directed the remaining hoses onto the library, but it was too late to save the old building. They were advised to concentrate on the surrounding buildings to prevent the fire from spreading.

Carter walked over to the ambo tent when he noticed Brooke standing there.

"Hey, are you ok?" she asked, concerned, as he walked closer.

His face was black, and he had a white ring around his eyes from the safety goggles he had taken off. He wore orange volunteer-unit overalls with a big number 5 on the back in red lettering.

"Yeah, I'll be right", he said as an ambo handed him a bottle of water. "What are you doing here? It's bloody dangerous, you should go," his tone was cold. She felt like he seemed angry at her.

"I heard about the fire and thought I'd bring some food and coffees for anyone who wanted it". Her food idea certainly wasn't unappreciated. Each of the ambos had a bacon and egg roll in their hands and countless others had a coffee. "Just trying to help".

Carter put his goggles and his hat back on "Seriously, you should go".

He threw the empty bottle to the side and walked back over to the hoses without saying another word. "You should go". He said again, turning back after a few steps.

"Don't take any notice of him, hun", a woman said as she stood watching him walk away. "I'm Sandra". Brooke read her badges on her uniform; she was a paramedic.

"Thanks, I'm Brooke".

Sandra smiled and drank some of the coffee she had taken from the box. "I know who you are,"

"Seems more people know me than me them lately". Brooke smiled.

"News travels fast around here, the café has been empty for years so it's nice to have it up and running again, I've heard great things about the food, oh, and the coffee ain't bad", she said taking another mouthful. "I'll drop in next shift when I'm on a break and grab a coffee, catch ya later, and thanks again for the coffee". Sandra smiled and walked back to the tent.

Carter kept turning to check if Brooke was still there. The stinging, tone in his eyes seemed unfriendly, she began to feel unwelcome and could feel herself starting to get upset. Talk about having the feeling you're being watched. She couldn't understand why it was such a problem for her to be there, she was not in any danger. They had been getting along so well. He kissed her. What was going on? Brooke cleared the empty cups and rubbish into a garbage bag she had bought. Moving all the remaining food and drinks into one box she walked the bag of rubbish and the empty box back to her ute and tossed them into the back seat. She walked around to the driver's side to see Carter standing at the driver's door leaning on the car.

"Excuse me", she said coldly as a lump built in her throat. There was no way she was going to give him the satisfaction of seeing her upset. She got in the driver's seat and shut the door.

"Brooke, give me a sec, please", he yelled through the closed window. She ignored him and he stepped out of the way as she started the engine, turned the car around and headed back to the café, leaving him standing in the middle of the road.

The café was full of lunch time customers when Brooke walked in the back kitchen door and over to the sink. She ran the cold water, splashing handfuls on her face and growled to herself in frustration.

"Who the hell does he think he is". She mumbled wiping her hands on a towel.

Dave stood on the other side of the prep bench looking at her.

"Everything all right?".

"Yep, I'm fine". She snapped and walked out the back door and across into the courtyard. She sat down hard on the wrought iron chair, Gambit quietly sat at her side, resting his head on her knee.

"I love you, Gam". She said as she rested her cheek on the top of his head. Leanne popped her head over the top of the gate.

"Can I come in?" Leanne opened the gate to Gambit's slobbery face rubbing all over her leg.

"Thanks, that's really nice of you", she said to Gambit, wiping her leg, taking the ball out of his mouth and throwing it down the courtyard for him. Leanne sat on the other chair and looked across at her.

"Everything ok?".

"Yeah, I'm fine, I took some rolls and coffee down to the firies and your brother pretty much said I wasn't welcome there".

"Ahhh, I'm sure he didn't mean it to come across that way, he can be very protective of people he cares about".

Brooke looked seriously at Leanne. "I don't understand why it was so bad for me to be there".

Gambit bought the ball back and dropped it at Leanne's feet, she picked it up with two fingers, the slobber dripping off, then threw it again.

"It's going to be a big loss for the town, they have a lot of activities for kids in the afternoons, like an afterschool care for parents who work, I overheard one of the ladies saying they were going to use the town hall in the interim so they can keep going".

Brooke shook off her own frustrations and thought on what Leanne had said.

"Let's do a fundraiser, maybe we could have Dave make some cookie boxes, all the proceeds going towards buying books". Brooke pondered.

"That's a great idea, we could put a donation box on the counter for customers who wish to give". Leanne added.

It wasn't long before Brooke had made social media posts and printed posters to put up in the café. One dollar from every coffee sold the following week would go to the fundraiser, also cookie boxes would be available to buy during the week, the proceeds of which would also go to the fund. She felt proud to be helping.

Brooke lay in bed that night barely able to sleep. So many thoughts and ideas going through her mind. Gambit lay on the end of her bed sleeping soundly. Carter played on her mind a lot. She wondered what could have happened for him to be so defensive. She was trying to remember what Leanne had said about cutting him some slack. The clock on the bedside table flicked over to midnight, that was the last time she remembered seeing as she drifted off to sleep.

Chapter 8

The locals responded well to Brooke's social media posts, and for the last 3 days the cookie boxes had sold out by lunchtime. Brooke had also started training Kim, the new waitress, at the start of the week. Probably throwing her in the deep end but how else does one learn.

Kim Sanderson was fresh out of high school; she was working hard doing an online course in horticulture. Brooke was happy to have the help now the café was starting to become busier during the lunch period.

Breakfast and lunch were fully booked out that day. Peter Archor came in just before close. Peter was the one person in town where, if you wanted to know something, 9 times out of 10 he would know.

"What are they doing with all the books that were on the street the other day?".

"There is a room at the Council Chambers they have been taken to, unfortunately they didn't save as many as they hoped, but the old newspaper archives they had stored was pretty much all saved".

"I wondered what those boxes were".

Peter took a bite from the carrot cake slice he was having with his coffee.

"Yeah, there is over 100 years of old papers there from The Emery Daily. I'll catch you tomorrow, Brooke, make sure you save me one of those cookie boxes, won't you".

"Sure thing, can you turn the sign around on your way out, thanks, Peter". Peter left and as asked turned the sign around on the front door.

Brooke counted the coins from the register as she heard the bell on the door ring. She looked up to see Carter standing shyly in the doorway.

"Can I come in?". He asked carefully. Brooke shrugged her shoulders and placed the coins back in the register. Carter was dressed in a nice dark pair of jeans and a check shirt. His hair was gelled and brushed nicely, no baseball cap in sight. "I was hoping that you would have dinner with me still, give me a chance to explain my behaviour the other day". Brooke contemplated saying no. "Please".

Brooke sighed hard, she remembered what Leanne had said, maybe she should give him a chance.

"Give me a bit to finish closing?" She asked softly.

Carter agreed to meet her at The Roundabout Hotel at 6pm. She smiled and kept counting coins as he left.

Brooke showered and fussed back and forth from the mirror trying on different outfits. After 5 different changes, she finally settled on a black pair of tailored pants, a one shoulder white top and red heels. She curled her hair and put a simple makeup on. She walked across the carpark and towards the main street. It wasn't a long walk to The Roundabout Hotel. She quietly pushed the main bar door open. The bar was packed, and she felt like every person turned to watch her come in. She was certainly over dressed for the location but held her head high in confidence. The bar was dated, had photos of the local football teams it sponsored on the walls and a small pokie room to one side with several televisions all with something different on, horse racing, football, and the local news channels. She would swear the carpet felt kind of sticky under her feet.

One familiar voice gave her comfort, sitting at the bar was the paramedic she met at the fire, Sandra.

"Wow you look absolutely beautiful, hun". Sandra said as she gave her a quick hug.

"Thank you, how have you been?"

"Good thanks, just had dinner with the family,". Brooke scanned the room for Carter. "Are you here for dinner?". The barman stood in front of her impatiently tapping his fingers on the bar waiting for her to stop talking to Sandra.

"Yes, I'm meeting someone".

"What can I get ya?". The publican was a large man, his belly hung over the top of his pants which fell down when he walked and every few steps he would pull back up way too far. He looked constantly sweaty, and she feared the stale beer smell was coming from him.

"I'll have a glass of Shiraz".

He gave her with a worried look. "I don't have fancy stuff, darl".

"That's fine, the house red will do".

Brooke saw Carter come in the back from what looked to be a beer garden, outdoor area. The relief she felt at seeing him was undeniable, the dread she was feeling, sitting at the bar and waiting for him was troubling.

"I'll get it, Luke", Carter said to the barman as he put a twenty dollar note on the bar. Carter passed the glass to her. There was definitely a feeling of being watched throughout the room.

"I'll catch you later, Sandra".

Sandra nodded as Carter placed his hand gentleman-like in the small of her back and led Brooke away.

"I hope you were not standing there long". Carter pulled out a chair for her at a little table in the corner of the dining area.

"Not at all". She took a large mouthful of her wine. The nerves suddenly crept up on her and she almost felt sick. They looked at the menu. It was a typical small town pub selection. Chicken snitty, steak, mixed grill, and a small selection of pizzas, all served with vegetables or salad and chips. There seemed to be more options in gravy types than meals.

Brooke ordered a chicken snitty with salad and Carter a steak and chips. He walked over to the window at the kitchen and placed their orders, in the meantime, she had downed the last of her wine. Carter came back to the table with a fresh glass and another beer for himself.

He was a bunch of nerves, to the point that his hands were shaking a little bit. Brooke could see the anguish on his face, he was struggling, and she felt the nervous pit in her stomach growing by the moment. She smiled with relief at the waitress who bought their meals over. Talk about fast service. Even with the lack of menu options, the meals were a generous size and absolutely delicious. Carter stopped in the middle of his meal and sighed.

"I have been needing to get a lot off my chest since the fire, I should have come and seen you sooner but wasn't sure what to say, my behaviour wasn't warranted towards you and I am sorry if I upset you". His tone was sincere, and it sounded like he had rehearsed that many times before she got there. She didn't know exactly what to say back to him and was struggling to finish her food due to her feeling so anxious.

"It's ok". That was it, it was all she could open her mouth to say. She was mortified but tried to reassure him. "I should have stayed away; you were right it was not the place to be".

She shuffled the salad around on her plate before finally putting her knife and fork down, then it came, the alcohol fuelled, verbal running writing, that leaps out of your mouth at moments like these which is usually followed by instant regret.

"Actually, no, I wasn't doing anything wrong, if anything I was doing the right thing with bringing the food down, whatever stick you had up your bum that day was nothing to do with me".

Carter leant back on his chair and folded his arms.

"It's really hard being the new person in town and trying to find my place, trying to fit in". She took a long mouthful of wine. "I want to do the right thing by the people here and you were not help……..".

"My wife died in a house fire". He interrupted her.

His deep monotone nearly knocked her off her chair. Brooke sat completely silent, looking down at her plate trying not to look at him, a tear fell onto her cheek and she sat quietly and listened.

"I was out driving a load of cattle, not sure exactly how it started but she was found slumped against the back door, trying to get out but couldn't get the door unlocked". Carter took a mouth full of his beer, he never took his eyes off her the entire time he was speaking but she struggled to look at him. "I would have been there if I didn't take the job that day, could have her saved her". Brooke finally looked up at him. His face spoke everything his mouth didn't.

"What was her name?". Brooke finally asked as she wiped her cheek with the back of her hand.

Carter sighed sadly, "Her name was Rachel".

Brooke sat quietly. She was ashamed of herself for the way she reacted. She drank the last of her wine and desperately tried to think of something to say that wouldn't sound as stupid as she felt.

"I'm sorry if I have ruined your night". He said softly.

Brooke searched her mind for answers, smiled and stood up and held out her hand.

"Do you like apple pie?"

Carter nodded. "Good, 'cause I made a fresh one this morning if you want to join me, I happen to know this little café that wouldn't mind a few after hours customers".

Carter looked relieved and took her hand without hesitation. Carter left his ute parked outside the pub and they walked down the main street still holding hands, not speaking, just being present in the moment. It was a cooler night than usual with the moon hanging high and full. Brooke opened the door and led him into the kitchen, pulling a stool over to the bench, prompting him to sit down. She opened the fridge and put a beautifully round pie on the bench, it had perfectly crisscrossed lines of pastry over the top, and you could see the shiny apple poking through the square holes. She placed a generous slice onto a plate and heated it up. Taking two spoons she pulled the garbage bin over to her side of the bench sitting on the lid, slid the plate into the middle and handed him a spoon. He looked impressed and happy which was nice. He dug the spoon in lifting a big chunk of pie and ice-cream. With little hesitation he shoved it in his mouth. She also took a spoonful.

"If heaven was a spoon, this would be it", he slumped down on the bench smiling.

"I'm glad you like it". Brooke smiled. "Just leave me some, hey". She laughed.

They spent hours talking about their favourite things. Brooke found herself liking him more as he spoke. He opened up a lot. Brooke suddenly yawned.

"I better get going. It's nearly midnight," he said looking at his watch.

Brooke regretfully nodded and led the way out the back kitchen door and down the path. He would need to walk back to the pub to get his car which, luckily, wasn't far. The night was still warm even though it was after midnight. The streetlights were dull, lighting the way back down the street.

"Thank you for the apple pie". The awkward, teenage fidgeting was obvious. She gave him a hug.

"Thank you for dinner". She whispered, breathing in deeply. His smell was almost intoxicating, goosebumps settled up her arms as she felt his hands resting on her waist. He kissed her on the cheek. Her heart was beating so fast she was positive he would be able to hear it. Brooke looked up into his brown eyes for a moment, he leant in nearly all the way, hovering his lips just above hers. She tilted her head up and went the rest of the way, she kissing him gently on the lips. Carter smiled; she loved his dimples as he did so. He ran his fingers up to her jaw, holding her face softly he kissed her again, moving his tongue around hers before resting his forehead on hers.

"Goodnight". He said softly and started to walk away still holding her hand until looking back towards her he gently let it go, walking off into the darkness.

Chapter 9

The rain was heavy and had not let up all night. The river was up and starting to lap higher up the banks. It was common at this time of year for seasonal rains, sometimes light showers, sometimes torrential downpours but non the less it was consistent.

Colin sat on the verandah as Brooke turned the sign around that morning. Even though it was raining it was still warm outside.

"Good mornin to you, Lass". He said cheerfully. "Think it's settled in for the long haul now". He said, watching the rain fall.

Brooke sat beside him. It was ages since she has had a chance to sit and talk to him and she was pleased to see him.

"Do you think the water will come up and into the park?".

"For sure, lass, I've seen it come right up ere to my feet". He said looking down at his stretched-out legs. "The rains will stay now, tis the season for it".

Brooke heard a bang, looking back over her shoulder to see the light fixture hanging in the centre of the room had fallen from the roof, breaking onto the floor.

"I'll be right back, did you want a cup of tea, Colin". She said as she hurried in the door to see hundreds of glass pieces across the floor. "I said did you want a cup of". She said walking back to the door to realise Colin was gone. "I guess not".

Leanne and Dave arrived sharing an umbrella after parking on the higher side of the carpark. Leanne gasped as she came in to see the light had fallen. Dave stepped over the broken pieces and into the kitchen coming back with a dustpan and broom.

"When did this happen?". Leanne asked, taking the broom off Dave, and sweeping the shards into a pile.

"Just now, I was out front talking to Colin when it suddenly fell".

Leanne looked at her confused. "Who?". Leanne swept the pieces into the dustpan as Dave held it still for her.

"Um, Colin, you know the old guy, he wears a kilt and sits in the park all the time".

Leanne thought carefully. Dave took the broom from Leanne.

"Can't say I've ever seen a guy in a kilt around here", Dave said, walking back into the kitchen.

Brooke felt even more confused. She shook it off looking up at the ceiling at the hole that was where the light once was.

"I'll call Carter, he will be able to have a look at that". Leanne said searching the contacts in her phone. Brooke walked back to the front door and looked out the window. It was strange that no one seemed to ever see Colin. She had spoken to him often since she came to town, it's weird to think a man in a kilt could go so unnoticed.

"Hey, can I ask you something while I have you on your own?". Brooke turned around and waited patiently.

"Sure, what's up".

Brooke motioned Leanne outside onto the verandah.

"Why didn't you tell me about Rachel the other day?". Leanne smiled and sighed.

"It wasn't my place to tell you, my brother is very closed when it comes to his feelings, he would have been angry at me if I had of shared that with you".

Brooke leaned forward and picked a piece of unoffending grass and started to pull it to pieces. "By that question, I gather he did tell you".

"Yeah, how long ago was it?". Brooke asked her, desperately trying to put more to the story.

"Going on 8 years now, he doesn't talk about it much, he holds himself responsible for her death, it wasn't his fault though."

Brooke threw the last of the grass into the garden and stood up to walk back inside.

"If it means anything, I see how much his face lights up when he sees you, saw it that first day he came in, I have not seen that light in him for a long time".

Brooke came back from making a catering delivery after the lunch rush to find Carter high on a ladder in the main room of the café, a pile of debris on the floor under it with customers stepping aside to give him space.

Ollie was standing in the kitchen doorway with his bucket of scraps.

"Hey Ollie, how many eggs do we have today?". Ollie came rushing over to her with a big smile.

"I have 14 eggs this week", he said proudly. "I lost 2 hens to a fox a few days ago".

Brooke rested her hand on his shoulder. "I'm sorry to hear that buddy". Brooke looked up the ladder at Carter.

"Is it bad up there?" She yelled.

Carter pulled what appeared to be a tartan drawstring bag from the hole.

"That is the same stuff as Colins kilt!" Ollie announced.

Brooke looked startled at the boy. "You know Colin? See, I knew I wasn't going mad".

Ollie nodded his head. "I leave him 3 eggs, every Monday on the way to school".

Brooke looked even more intrigued than before as she held the little drawstring bag. Carter and Brooke stood at the counter as she opened the bag. She gently tipped the contents out onto the glass. Out came a beautiful old pocket watch, it has carvings of mountains on it and as Carter pushed the little button, the clasp slowly opened, on the inside the cover, an engraved inscription read "With all my love, Edith" there was also a gold nugget, about the size of a grape attached to a necklace, several old Scottish shillings, one in particular that dated back to 1902 and a big key, like the kind from an old, heavy wooden door.

"Edith is his wife". Ollie said after seeing the inscription.

Brooke stared at him for quite some time before her mouth finally found words. "Whose wife?", she asked intently.

Ollie seemed surprised that she was asking.

"Colin's of course".

Brooke looked at Carter speechless.

"I better get going, dad will wonder where I am". Ollie left with his bucket of chook scraps; it was like he wasn't at all concerned about what they had found.

"Ollie, where do you leave the eggs, you know, for Colin?". Ollie turned back to face her as he crossed the room to go home.

"In the letter box at the side of Dad's shop, Colin said he didn't want to come inside so I just leave them there". Ollie smiled, like a typical teen and off he went, head in the clouds.

"Who is Colin?" Carter asked her.

Brooke held the watch in her hand as she relayed the stories of their meetings over the time she had been at Emery.

Carter looked deep in thought. "I also can't remember ever knowing a man named Colin, but I know who would". It was a man named Gordon Cranston, he was the curator of the museum and the Mayor. The museum had a lot of history about the gold rush and the old timers.

"Do you want me to come with you, we can go tomorrow if you like". Brooke agreed and put the pouch in the top drawer under the counter.

It was starting to get late, and the rain was still falling heavily. Brooke stood at the base of the ladder with a glass of red and Carter with a beer waiting on the table. She watched him install the new light into the place where the old one had been as Gambit slept on the floor near the kitchen door.

"I do charge after hours rates you know". He said, smiling as he came down the ladder and stopped at the bottom in front of her. She found herself holding her breath, he leant forward and kissed her. She felt the hairs on her arms stand on end.

"Is there anything you can't do?". She observed, as he folded it, leaning it against the wall. She couldn't help but smile at him, he really was a sweet guy and always was there when she needed something.

"Haha, I can't dance".

Brooke's eyes lit up with a random idea. She ran quickly out to the kitchen and came back with a small speaker. She flicked the lights off, so the only ones left on were the veranda lights, giving a dim, moody pattern of shadows across the room. She put the speaker on the table and blue-toothed her phone to play music. She put on a slow song called Carried Away by George Strait, turned towards him, and held out her hands.

"Come on". Brooke said softly.

Carter shook his head and laughed it off, deep down he was terrified. Brooke walked across the room towards him, her eyes fixed on his, there was no way she was taking no for an answer. She knelt down in front of him, close enough that he could smell the sweetness of her perfume and held out both of her hands. "Come on". She whispered softly.

Carter couldn't do anything to control his hands, they had a mind of their own and reached out to hers before he had a chance to take control. She walked him into the middle of the room.

"I really can't dance". He said nervously, looking down at the floor trying to shy away from her, he was visibly scared. She put his hands around her waist and looked into his eyes.

"Neither can I," she whispered. She put her arms around his neck, taking the lead and the pressure from him. She could feel his arms wrapping tighter around her as they swayed side to side. She rested her cheek against his. They danced as the song played. The shadows across the room created magic she couldn't have imagined. She could feel across his body every nervous breath he took; goosebumps ran up her arms. She ran her fingers up the back of his neck and into his hair, he lifted his face to look into her eyes. She gently leaned in and kissed his cheek. He found himself letting his inhibitions slide away for a moment and was completely engulfed in her energy. He ran his hand along her jaw pulling her closer and kissed her. It was gentle but also fierce, it was deep and passionate. He ran his tongue over hers gently but also like they could have pushed each other to the limit with just that single kiss. She could barely keep herself together, his hands entwined in her hair as he kissed her cheek. The song came to an end, and he took a step back still holding her hands.

"See, you can dance," she whispered, feeling a little flustered.

"I better get going". Carter let go of her hands and packed up his tools, picked up his ladder and carried it under one arm outside to his ute. Brooke had that churning feeling form deep in her stomach that she may have overstepped just now. Suddenly the tension in the air seemed thick.

"I'll pick you up in the morning, if you still want me to come see Gordon with you". He said to her, standing on the veranda.

Brooke felt a bit of relief, surely if he was having any hard feelings he wouldn't want to see her again tomorrow.

"I'd like that". She walked him to the door. "Thank you for coming after hours, be sure to send me an invoice won't you". She said trying to ease the tension. Carter smiled that cheeky smile and hugged her. His arms felt strong around her, he leant in and kissed her cheek, looking right into her eyes, she swallowed hard as he whispered.

"It's on the house".

Chapter 10

Brooke heard the bell of the door jingle from the kitchen. Her heart was racing, and she felt nervous. Carter was on her mind, it was pretty much all she could think about, she had not seen him for a few days, and it was starting to drive her a bit mad. Maybe she did push it a bit far making him dance. Thinking it would be him there for his Black with no sugar, she leaped out of the kitchen, she saw him standing there. If it was possible to physically evaporate into thin air from shock, she would have done so right then. Standing at the counter wasn't Carter, it was her dad.

"Dad!". Brooke was frozen to the spot. Fear was her first response; she had not seen her father in three years.

"I'll have a piccolo", he said sternly after looking up at the menu. If she thought the moment couldn't get any worse, she was wrong. The bell on the door jingled again, looking up, this time it *was* Carter. She could feel the colour draining from her face. Carter instantly sensed the energy in the room as soon as he saw the man in a business suit and brief case standing at the counter. What was he thinking? What was he going to say? She thought quickly and sprang around the counter to Carter before he got even halfway across the room. She wanted nothing more than for him to pick her up and carry her away.

"Can we do this later?" Brooke looked at him with the world on her shoulders. "I have had something come up".

Carter looked over her shoulder at the man standing at the counter who was ignoring him completely.

"No worries, shoot me a text when you're free". The moment she was dreading most was right in front of her as he leant in and kissed her on the cheek. She smiled awkwardly.

Carter could sense the urgency about her reaction. "I'll leave you to it".

Brooke hated watching him leave, with some relief Leanne arrived for the breakfast run. Brooke walked back to the counter. Her Father looking less than impressed.

"I'll take it over there". He said pointing to the table in the corner where Colin liked to sit. Leanne put her apron on and stood next to her at the coffee machine.

"What's going on?". Brooke made him a Piccolo and gently put it on a small saucer with a coin sized cookie she added to every order.

"That, unfortunately, is my dad". Brooke walked around to the front of the counter picked up the coffee and walked it across the room, carefully putting it down on the table. He sat typing on his ipad, his glasses sitting on the tip of his nose, just like Erin wore hers. She just stood there. Waiting before she finally opened her mouth.

"What are you doing here, Dad?".

"Your sister told me about how she came all the way out here and transformed your new business, so I thought, since you can't find the time to call to tell me, I'd just come to look for myself, she did a good job by looks".

Brooke looked down at the floor and pursed her lips. Of course, Erin had told him that she saved the day, wouldn't expect anything else really, she always loved daddy's attention.

"Don't worry I won't be staying, not really the kind of town I want to stay in too long". His arrogance infuriated her. Why was he even here, Brooke knew it wasn't for anything productive, that's for sure, he was there to tell her she is wrong and turn his nose up like he always did.

"I am on my way to Townsville actually, have to be in court there in the morning".

She glanced across the room out the window to see a BMW parked out front.

"You drove here?". She asked in utter disbelief. He looked over his glasses at her, they were still perched on his nose, the unimpressed resting bitch face that Erin constantly had, she obviously got off their father.

"Wanted to give my new car a good run".

"What exactly do you want, Dad?". Brooke leant back on the chair and crossed her arms. "You drove 9 hours out of your way to come here. Why? I know it wasn't to play happy family, that's for sure".

Brooke and her dad clashed over everything and had done so for years. Erin was the favourite, and he gave her the world, but Brooke felt like she had to work so much harder to get positive acknowledgment from him and even then, he still was never happy. He saw her as an interruption to his lifestyle. It didn't surprise her that he would drive so far for nothing else but to give his disapproval. He did right by her mother with child support when she was a child but wanted little to do with her.

"I wanted to see where my money had gone, since you did buy this with my money, technically".

She knew what he was saying, he referred to the fact that she sold the Mercedes he bought her, again, Erin would have told him.

"Also, to give you this, I am the executor of the will so by law I need to fulfill the clients wishes".

He passed her an official orange envelope, a4 size. It was sealed and had her name written on it, her father's law firm credentials on the top corner. She opened it and pulled out the thick stapled collection of papers. It was a will, her grandfather's to be exact. She never met her grandfather on her mother's side. Earnest Henry Kensington, last will and testament the paper read. She read over the points stated until she came to her name. He had left her mother a substantial amount of money. After her death it was changed so his only grandchild would receive the inheritance, that grandchild was her. Attached to the will was a cheque in the amount of one hundred and fifty thousand dollars. Brooke sat speechless and in disbelief at what she was reading but then the realisation set in. He didn't come here to see her or to look around at what she had achieved, he wasn't proud of her nor happy for her new business, he came for nothing else but to give her that because it was his 'job' to do so. Despite them not getting along over the years and her being shunned by him most of her life, deep down she hoped that maybe, just maybe he might, even a little bit, love her. He took his glasses off and placed them back in the case, stood up and buttoned his jacket. He had no emotion to his face.

"My work here is done. Goodbye, Brooke".

He was gone quicker than he came. He showed no warmth towards her which she had accepted years ago but there was that little part in her heart that hoped perhaps he would walk in and wrap his arms around her and tell her how proud he was. He left without another word, no hug or feeling. Just walked out.

Carter headed into the café for his usual coffee later that afternoon to find Leanne.

"We're closed, Bro". Carter looked at his watch not realising the time, looked around looking like he had the weight of the world on his shoulders. "What's going on? And don't tell me nothing cause I can see right through you". She bossed him just like a big sister would.

"Was hoping to see Brooke".

"She is out delivering orders". Leanne watched the expression of his face change. "I know what is wrong, you need to stop it, I can see it all over your face every time you're here how much you like her".

Carter shook the comment off.

"You are allowed to be happy, Carter, you have to let the wall down". Leanne watched as he headed for the door. "Rach would want you to be happy," Leanne yelled across the room at him. Carter turned to look at his sister and opened his mouth to say something but changed his mind. The door slammed behind him as he left.

Brooke had a shower and sat on the couch in just a loose button up shirt and denim shorts, looking at the cheque. Earnest Henry Kensington. She had vague memories of her mum calling him Grandpa Ernie, but she never met him. She heard the gate open, and footsteps crossed the courtyard to the door. Gambit darted across to the door wagging his tail furiously. She looked up to see Carter standing at the screen door.

"Can I come in?". Brooke nodded, putting the cheque back in the envelope.

As usual gambit plopped himself at Carter's feet, legs in the air, expecting a belly rub. Carter could see she was upset, he sat beside her and put his arm around her. He had been thinking about what happened between them for a few days. He couldn't help but feel guilty that she made him feel alive again and it scared him.

"Are you ok?"

She nodded. "That was my father,".

"Is he not staying?"

Brooke shifted herself on the couch to sit facing him cross legged. And told him about her childhood and how her life had been after her mother died. She started to cry. Carter sat and listened; he held her hand but never interrupted her. She leant her head on his shoulder and sobbed as she told him about her mother.

Carter had been fighting his feelings towards her. It was something he had not felt since his wife died, that little flutter of nervous butterflies inside whenever she was close to him. He even felt it first time he stepped into the café, to see that ignorant city chick. He wanted to be around her, he wanted to kiss her, he wanted the feelings he had growing to never fade. The sexual tension between them was electric.

Brooke struggled to keep hold of her emotions. She stood up and let Gambit outside, then turned to find him standing right behind her, taking her hand, and pulling her in closer. He touched her face, wiped a tear away with his thumb. He kissed her. It was soft but she could feel the passion as the kiss intensified. She kissed him deeper, her hands moving up his back under his shirt to feel the heat of his smooth skin. She felt as light as air, she ran her hands up under his shirt touching his chiselled, muscular chest. Carter suddenly pulled himself away, breathing heavily, looking into her eyes.

"I'm sorry". He looked flustered and that pain she saw come across his eyes made her heart ache.

She stood there not knowing what to say. What was she going to do, she had feelings for him, they got deeper every time she saw him, every time she kissed him.

He kissed her softly on the cheek as she grabbed his hand, not letting him walk away. "I'm sorry, Brooke, I have to go". Carter touched the side of her face with his hand and quietly left. She rubbed her arms as goosebumps prickled her skin.

Chapter 11

Brooke went about her day trying to put Carter out of her mind, she had not seen him in a few days, and he had not come in for coffee at all. The rain had let up which sent a good vibe through the town. It was Saturday afternoon when Leanne and Kim counted the orders for the day. 25 for breakfast, 40 for lunch and 295 coffees and teas. That's not bad at all.

Brooke looked at her phone to see a text from Carter. He asked if she wanted to come with him for a night camping. She was hesitant but said yes. Leanne smiled as she watched Brooke float around the room.

"You're happier today". There was no way that Leanne didn't know what was happening with Carter.

"Today may be a good day after all". Brooke continued to scamper about, tidying up and wiping tables.

"I'm off, I'll deliver these orders on my way home". Leanne said.

Brooke locked the front door after everyone had left. She put Gambit on his lead and carried a small bag out to the carpark. Carter was sitting in his ute waiting for her. He got out. As she got closer, her heart beat faster. She was nervous. He opened the back door for Gam, and she climbed up into the passenger side.

"Where are we going?". She asked. She could barely sit still. She was so anxious but excited at the same time.

"You will need to wait and see". Carter pulled into the servo to fill up. She couldn't help but feel like people were looking at her. Carter came back out and handed her a bottle of lemonade.

They drove down the highway for 15 minutes before turning off onto a dirt road that had deep tyre grooves filled with mud and water. Her stomach turned and a feeling of dread came over her as she looked down the road. "Are we going down there?" Stupid question, of course they were. He smiled that cheeky grin at her before putting his foot down. Brooke held on to the door with one hand and the seat with the other trying not to show him how terrified she was. The ute slid around in the mud like it was on ice, mud and dirty water sprayed up the sides and onto the windscreen, the wipers flicked on and pushed the dark brown, chunky water of to the side. It felt like they were on this track for 10 years in her mind, finally he pulled the ute up out of the mud and up a rocky incline and into a clearing.

"Here we are", he laughed at her holding on to the seat before getting out, Gambit flew out the door keen to explore.

She slowly got out, still feeling her hands shaking, and looked around. There was a small cabin nestled between a few big trees. There was a section in front of the cabin that was grass. Carter took her hand and led her up the stairs and onto the little porch. A swinging chair hung from the roof on one end. From the porch, the view across the mountains was as far as you could see. The trees gave a green spray of colour across the red dirt and rocks, it was truly beautiful.

"What do you think?" Carter asked.

"It's beautiful, what Is this place?"

Carter ran his hand along the beam above the door to retrieve the key.

"It's my home away from home, I call it the hideaway, somewhere I come when life feels heavy". He pushed the door open. Inside there was one big room with a bathroom off to the side. There was a big bed made from raw, uncut logs in the centre and a small kitchen on the left side also made from timber. A wooden fireplace on the right with a black metal chimney up into the ceiling, it was rustic but yet serene.

"Do you come here often?".

"Used to, not so much anymore, I just thought I'd show you another part of me, I guess. I used to dream about building a beautiful big homestead here, have horses and chickens".

Brooke smiled, she always saw herself living a carefree life with lots of animals, could this man be any more perfect.

"Make yourself at home and I'll bring in our stuff".

Gambit took up residence on the porch like he was king. Carter bought in their bags and the bags of essentials for their stay. "Are you up for a walk? I want to show you something".

Brooke took his hand as Gambit followed and he led her down the hill towards the creek, she stepped down several wooden stairs to the bottom where there was a wooden deck, the edge sat on the side of a deep section of water so clear you could count the pebbles on the bottom.

"This is amazing, did you build it?". Brooke took off her shoes and sat on the edge with her feet in the water. Carter sat beside her.

"When Rachel died, I spent a lot of time here, built the cabin with a good mate of mine from Geraldton, Derek, he spent a few weeks here making sure I didn't unalive myself". Carter shrugged his shoulders. Brooke touched his leg in comfort. "Built the deck a few months ago, actually, popped out earlier in the week for a few days to put a coat of stain on before it started raining again, wasn't in a good head space for a long time and this was a way I could always escape".

"What's going there?" Brooke pointed out the pile of wood with a tarp over it to the side, "Are you building something else?"

Carter smiled. "I was going to put a roof over this, but I got distracted a few months back by city chick stuck on the side of the road, never really got around to it after that".

Brooke laughed. She was never going to live that moment down that was sure.

"I would love to help you build something one day". Brooke felt happy. Happiness comes in so many forms but sitting there with him she felt happy.

He took her hand in his. "I'm sorry I ran out on you the other day, it wasn't anything you did, I assure you, it was just my own insecurities I guess".

Brooke slumped her shoulders down and ran her hand along the top of his. She didn't know what to say, she was confused about what was happening between them but didn't want to push him away.

"It's ok".

"I..just..". He struggled to find the right words. "I have feelings for you, and it scares the hell outta me because I....". He let go of her hand and rubbed his hands over his face, taking off his baseball cap he scratched the back of his head and sighed heavily. "I'm scared to let myself, I'm...".

Brooke leant forward and kissed his cheek, trying to comfort him, she could feel the anguish listening to his voice.

He looked into her eyes. "Truthfully, I'm falling for you, but I'm scared to lose someone again".

Brooke felt her eyes well up. "I'm not going anywhere". She wrapped her arms around his neck and held him. Out of nowhere water engulfed the air in a tidal wave and landed all over them. Gambit had taken a flying leap off a rock and into the deep pool in front of them. Brooke and Carter laughed so hard their stomachs hurt. Talk about making an entrance to break the moment.

Brooke had a shower while Carter washed up the dishes from dinner. She sat on the end of the bed with just her usual bedtime button up shirt and small running shorts. The night had fallen quickly out there, and it was dark, darker than she had ever seen, there were no streetlights and no noise. Gambit was sleeping soundly, and his nasal snore was the only noise that filtered through the room. She sipped a glass of wine. There was less tension, she felt like there was a weight lifted off Carter's shoulders. After he showered, he pulled on an old shirt and a pair of trackie pants and sat on the lounge across from her. Brooke felt the nerves creeping up on her more and more. She stood and went to walk over to refill her glass when he reached out and grabbed her hand, taking the glass and putting it on the floor. The moon was brighter here than in town and it gave a cool glow and ambience to the room.

The energy between them had been building over the last weeks. He finally let himself into the moment, and without hesitating, he pulled her down onto his lap, her legs straddled on each side and kissed her. His hands entwined in her hair as the kiss intensified. He kissed her neck as she tilted her head towards him. She slid his shirt over his head, his muscular arms and chest nearly took her breath away. He unbuttoned her shirt letting it slip onto the floor. She had no bra on, her nipples hard as he gently ran his fingers over them. He lifted her like she weighed as much as a feather, laying her down on the pillows. He took off his pants and reached forward and pulled off her shorts kissing down her stomach and to her inner thigh. She arched her back as his tongue moved gently around her clit, then harder and more intense. Brooke reached down, he was hard, and she squeezed gently. He let out a moan, lifted his head and moved up, looking at her, his brown eyes melted her, he kissed her deeply, his hand moving down to play again, making her wriggle around under him until she couldn't wait any longer. Brooke rolled him over and gently eased herself onto his near throbbing erection. She rocked herself back and forth slowly, he moved his hands down her back and held onto her, guiding her faster and deeper. She rested her forehead on his, they breathed together as she let out a soft but sharp breath as she came. He lifted her up so she was leaning over the back of the couch and entered her from behind. Harder and faster, he reached under her and pinched her nipples, he couldn't hold back any longer, it was intense as he let himself go. She raised her body up as he came turning her head back towards him, he kissed her cheek as they dropped into a heap on the cushions. She lay on top of him, her hair spread out over his chest. He ran his fingers up and down her back. She could hear his deep heartbeat as she lay there in his arms, feeling completely safe.

Chapter 12.

The rain had been unforgiving for the last 3 days. It was usual for the wet season to have monsoon like rains, but it was a bit early for that so the rain lasting so long was a bit unusual. Sometimes it was light showers but other times it was week-long downpours. The weather report spoke of abnormal weather events being a result of global warming which she didn't know much about. The water was through the park as the river had broken its banks and it was starting to edge towards the café carpark. Brooke and Carter waited in the waiting room at the Emery Museum for Gordon. Around the walls were old photographs of how the town looked hundreds of years ago but one that caught her eye over all the others was a man standing in front of what is now her café with a gold nugget the size of a football.

"That was the biggest nugget ever found in this region, they called it The Frankston Nugget," a voice came as Brooke turned to see the mayor and curator. "My name's Gordon. How are you going, Carter?" he asked politely, shaking Brooke's hand. Brooke pointed to the photo, "That's my place", she said proudly. "Ahh yes, back in the days when the gold rush was on it was a few different places, post office, general store, and as you know it now of course, Brooke's Place". Gordon pointed to the description under the photo. The photo was taken in 1899, had bales of wool behind the man holding the nugget and a bullock train in the background beside the store. "The gold rush for Emery started back in 1860 and went right through to 1912, It was a very rich town back in the day, not much gold found now though, doesn't stop people from trying". He led them down a corridor to a room with archives written on the door.

"Carter gave me a brief gist of what you're looking for so I have had bought over from the council chambers a selection of newspapers ranging from 1920 to 2005, hopefully you can find what you're looking for here".

Gordon excused himself and left them to the pile of boxes of papers stacked neatly against the wall. Brooke felt exhausted looking at them.

Carter and Brooke went through box after box over the next few hours. Not much was helping until they reached a box labelled 1940-45. Carter read through a few before placing a very worn newspaper open at page 5 on the table in front of her.

The headline was about local marriages. She followed the list down to find a small paragraph stating the marriage the new of Mr and Mrs Crawford. Mrs Crawford wore a white lace gown and carried a posy of red flowers she read. Her mouth dropped open as she continued. Mr Crawford, a Scottish immigrant, will reside here in Emery as the new Barber.

"Oh my god". Brooke exclaimed loudly as she started to put the pieces together. She started opening boxes from 1970-75. She remembered Leanne saying that Mr Crawford bought his wife the café for their 30th wedding anniversary. It wasn't long before Brooke slumped herself down onto the floor beside the box in complete shock. She was holding a paper dated Monday, 25th of September 1974. The Blue bell café was opened by Mr and Mrs Crawford. The article had a picture of a middle-aged couple standing outside the café. She sat on the floor and stared at none other than Colin. Mr Colin Crawford. He wore the same kilt and knee-high socks that she had seen him in.

"I don't believe it". Brooke thought about the times that she had seen Colin; he wore the same outfit every time she had seen him. No one remembered him being in the café that day, he never ate the scones, and he said on the first day she met him that if she ever needed anything he lived upstairs above the Barber shop.

Brooke and Carter photocopied the pages and went back to the café. They didn't say a single word to each other the whole way back. Brooke was still in shock. Could Colin be the reason people had not shown interest in buying the café? Because they thought it was haunted, why is it that she had never felt that from being there? Not once did she hear odd noises or see anything strange, and most of all why is it that Ollie can see him?

They sat in the kitchen after close and laid it all out on the table. By the end of the story, Dave and Leanne were as deeply invested in the mystery as she was.

"Why is he still here, didn't you say he drowned?" Leanne thought on what she had said back when Brooke first bought the café.

"I heard the story over the years of Mr Crawford taking his boat down to the river, he was known around town for doing it often". Leanne poured her and Brooke a glass of wine. "It was assumed he drowned 'cause he went missing while fishing in his boat".

"But they never recovered a body?". Brooke added. "Or found his boat".

Dave sat quietly before adding something of his own to the theory.

"My aunt was a tarot reader, she used to tell me, when I was younger, that sometimes souls get trapped here while ever they have unfinished business, maybe that's relevant to this situation". Dave said.

"But why can Ollie see him". Brooke asked.

An expression came over Leanne's face, she seemed to have a lightbulb moment.

"Look, it says here in the marriage notice that Mr Crawford would reside in Emery as the new barber, I'm pretty sure that Peter Archor Real estate was the barber shop back then".

Brooke sat back against the wall with her mouth open. "There is a photo on the wall when you go in the door of what the building looked like back then, maybe call over and have a look at it".

Brooke pushed through the door of Peter Archor Real estate as they opened the next morning. Peter greeted her as she came in with a solid handshake and big smile as she handed him a coffee.

"You sure can read minds, thank you," he said taking the coffee with a giddy little boy smile. "What can I do you for, Miss Brooke". He cheerfully took a long mouthful of his coffee.

"Leanne said you had a photo of this building back in gold rush days, I was hoping I could have a look at it". Peter's eyes lit up. There was nothing more this man loved to do than talk about the history of the town, alongside Gordon, he was Vice President of the History Preservation society in Emery and very proud.

"Oh yes, over here", he led Brooke to a black and white photograph on the wall. "Back in the day this was a barber shop, and before that, it was the local office for Cobb and Co. Back in the late 1800s, they used to pull the old coach up out front". Brooke looked intently at the photo. It was old and not as clear as modern day photos.

"Do you know much about the barber shop?". Peter pointed to another photo off to the side near the window. Brooke looked at it carefully and again there he was, Colin. "This man, do you know much about him?".

Peter smiled and motioned Brooke to take a seat and sat down beside her. "Mr Crawford was a Scottish fellow, came over on a ship called The Grand Princess as an orphan when he was round 10 years old. He was adopted by an Australian family, moved to Emery and married an

Australian woman when he was 20, tried his hand at gold mining early on like a lot of folks did back then but never hit the mother lode". Peter said in an exaggerated tone.

Brooke was completely invested in hearing the story and Peter enjoyed telling it. "He ran the Barber shop, I'd say, for a good 30 years, was in his 80's when he went missing, Silly old bugger went fishing one day and was never seen again". Peter raised the bottom of his cup high in the air drained the last of the coffee.

"Edith died bout 4 years ago. They had a boy, think his name was Thomas but he went off to the Army when he was just 16, not sure what happened to him."

Brooke looked at Colin one more time, in this photo, like the others she had seen, he wore his kilt.

"Oh, Peter, does Ollie leave eggs in the letter box each week?"

Peter laughed. "Yeah, he started doing that years ago, I just take them out and put them back in the fridge, not sure why he does it, makes him happy, so I don't say anything".

"Thank you, Peter, you have helped a lot today," Brooke glanced back at the barbershop photo before letting herself out.

She walked back along the main street looking at the old shops. Each of those probably had an extraordinary story to tell, much like Colin's. She had so much information but still no real answers as to why he was still around.

It was starting to become an afternoon ritual, gathering around the kitchen, and talking about the mystery of Colin. Brooke shared with everyone what she had discovered at the real estate. Leanne rested her chin on her hand lost in thought.

Chapter 13

Brooke woke in the early hours, she lay in bed for a few minutes listening, not sure if it was the rain on the roof or if she really heard something. There it was again. Gambit, by now, was up at the front door sniffing the ground. Brooke parted the curtain carefully and peered out into her courtyard. Nothing there. There it was again; she couldn't quite put her finger on what the noise was exactly. She gently opened the wooden door, she could hear it more clearly now, it sounded like someone was in the kitchen at the café. She hushed Gambit, he was a good boy and crept across the courtyard after her until she raised her hand, and he sat still. She slowly opened the gate; she could see the back kitchen door across the path. Picking up a large stick she crept across the path one foot at a time to the window next to the back door. There was a torch light moving around in the kitchen, she watched them leave and go into the main café.

Brooke wasn't planning to march herself in and save the day, kneeling down under the window at the back of the café she called the police. Then waited as they instructed but couldn't hear them anymore, so much for not trying to save the day, she opened the back door. There was someone in the kitchen. They were in black and wore their hood down over their face. The startled intruder struck Brooke in the face knocking her to the ground before running out the back door with Gambit running after him. Whoever else was in the café also took off out the front door, smashing the glass as they ran. The paddy wagon pulled up, the red and blue flashing lights bounced off the walls into the carpark just as the man ran out the front door, one policeman took off running after the intruder leaving Constable McDonald on his own, he drew his gun, yelled out alerting anyone to his presence and walked carefully inside over the smashed glass. He walked slowly across the room to the main counter, the drawer under the register was pulled out on the floor, its contents spread across the floorboards, he heard a noise in the kitchen, he edged closer to the kitchen door and yelled loudly.

"Police, anyone here". He yelled again.

"James".

He heard a whisper behind the door. He holstered his gun when he saw Brooke sitting on the ground leaning against the kitchen bench. She was bleeding from a cut just under her eyebrow. Her eye had started to swell up and was barely open. The Young constable that James had on duty with him turned the lights on as he came into the room, he's had no luck with the escaped perp, so he came back. He saw Brooke sitting on the floor with James, kneeling in front of her.

James pushed the button on his shoulder mic, "Emery 34 to VKG", he said clearly into his microphone.

"VKG to Emery 34, go ahead" the voice said back.

"Emery 34 require immediate ambulance assistance to my location, one 27 yr old female, conscious with a laceration to left eye."

"VKG to Emery 34, copy that, ambulance inbound".

Brooke fumbled around with her phone and managed to dial Carter's number and James could hear him yelling "Hello" as she sat incoherent on the floor.

"Hello, this is Constable James McDonald to whom am I speaking?"

James heard Carter on the other end of the phone and relayed breifly what had happened.

"He is on his way, Brooke". James reported, passing back her phone.

James grabbed a t towel from the rail near the sink and held against the bleeding.

"Gam, where is Gam?" She kept asking over and over as the ambulance arrived. Carter slid his ute sideways into the carpark not long after and busted his way through the door. The ambulance officer put a dressing on her head and helped her to her feet. She sat slowly down on the stretcher.

"Brooke, it's me", he said holding her hand. Brooke squeezed his hand tightly.

"Gam, he ran off, where is he?".

Carter was torn between going with Brooke to the hospital and Gambit being missing. He scanned his phone for his sister's number, she sleepily answered.

"Find Gam, Carter". Brooke said as they wheeled her out of the kitchen.

Carter found his head and his heart going at it like a boxing match. One minute he decided to go with her, the next he was going to look for the dog. As they loaded Brooke into the ambulance he finally succumbed to her wishes and agreed to look for the dog. He watched her drive away as Leanne arrived still dressed in her pyjamas.

The Police taped off the café and had Leanne lock the door. James explained to Leanne that the café would have to be closed until a team of could come from the city to fingerprint and collect any evidence after which business could resume. No one would be able to enter until then. Carter drove around the streets looking for Gambit. There was no sign of him at all. The streets were quiet. He went to the hospital to check on Brooke, he was never going to find him in the dark. Carter was let into Emergency to see Brooke. The nurse directed him to bed 2. Peering through the gap in the curtain he could see she was laying on her side staring into thin air.

"Hey". He whispered as he pushed the curtain aside. Brooke smiled sleepily. The pain medication had certainly kicked in. Her face was even more bruised than when he last saw her, she had 5 stitches slightly under her brow, and her eye was swollen shut, she started to cry when she saw him.

"It's ok". He took her hand and sat on the chair beside the bed.

"Did you find Gam?". He looked at her pain-filled face and regretted coming.

"I drove around but it's too dark, I thought I'd try again, soon, when the sun comes up." He kissed the back of her hand. "I just wanted to come check on you, I have been so worried", he whispered, looking up to realise she was asleep. He just sat there for a while and watched her; he couldn't deny his feelings had grown. They took off now, like wildfire, he was a goner the day he walked into the Blue Bell and realised she was the new owner. A clueless city chick had turned his world upside down, he never thought anyone would make him feel this way again, he couldn't imagine life without her.

As promised, Carter drove around as soon as the sun came up. The rain had come back like clockwork and was steady and relentless. It wasn't long before news spread through the town of what had happened. Ollie convinced his dad to give him a day off school and walked with his umbrella through the streets calling Gambit's name. Leanne stayed at Brooke's place, sitting in kitchen leaving the gate open in case he came home.

By lunchtime three bunches of flowers had been delivered from locals hearing about the robbery. Dave picked up Brooke from hospital later in the afternoon. She had a concussion but in time her face would heal. Dave opened the door for her as she slowly walked in.

"No sign of Gam", she signed. He wasn't one to run away, he was always a good boy and stayed close by her side. He always came home, which made her wonder if he may be injured somewhere.

"Carter has been out since daybreak looking for him". Leanne reassured her. "He will come home".

Ollie knocked quietly on the door, Leanne let him in, he folded his umbrella up and left it against the front wall. He looked like he had the world on his shoulders as he handed Brooke a blue and gold Collar. It was Gambit's.

"I found this a few blocks over in Hampton Street, no sign of him though". Brooke held the collar, looking at it carefully. "I can keep looking if you like?" Ollie asked thoughtfully.

"It's ok Ollie you should head home, I'll let you know if he comes home". Brooke shook Ollie's hand which gave a sense of relief to the boy as he left.

Brooke lay in Carter's arms unable to sleep. She couldn't stop thinking about Gambit. The rain was still falling. It was 4 days of it now, maybe he got disoriented and is hiding in someone's shed or something. What could the men in the café have been looking for. According to police they didn't tear the place apart, instead being very specific to where they had been looking, the draw under the register was the only thing touched. They pulled it out and spread its contents on the floor as if they were looking for something. The sound of the rain eventually put her to sleep. There was something calming about listening to the rain fall.

The water was gently edging towards the café carpark as day 5 of rain begun.

Brooke, Carter, Dave, and Leanne sat around Brooke's dining table. The news that morning had issued a flood warning for Emery and surrounds as the river rose. The café had never flooded before according to Leanne, she had lived in Emery for most of her life.

Brooke remembered that Colin had said to her, that day sitting on the verandah, that he remembered it at his feet.

"The water got up to the front door once but never inside," Leanne mentioned. Brooke wondered if she should put some sandbags in front of the door just in case. The café had been shut for 4 days, finally the forensic team had finished up their job inside yesterday but due to the rain Brooke thought it would be best to stay shut until the river peaked which according to the news would be later that afternoon.

"I also had a thought last night lying in bed". Brooke mentioned suspiciously. "I was thinking 'bout how they didn't completely trash the café, they only went to that drawer".

Leanne looked deep in thought, listening.

"There isn't anything in that drawer, though, except pens and spare menus," Leanne mumbled.

Brooke stood up and walked to the tv cabinet, opened the lid of a decorative box Erin had given her and pulled out the tartan pouch they found in the roof of the cafe.

"Maybe, what they were looking for 'was' in there once." Brooke bought it back over and tipped out the contents again on the table. Again, there was a pocket watch, a gold nugget on a necklace, coins, and an old key. They all looked at the items quietly, lost in their imaginations of why these objects were in the pouch.

"What does this open?" Brooke asked the group as she held the key.

Suddenly Carter's head turned, and he shushed everyone with a finger to his mouth.

"Listen".

It was a faint noise, but it was definitely there. It was a dog barking. Everyone in the room leapt to their feet and one by one ran out the door not caring about the rain. Carter busted the gate open which led them out in the carpark. The barking was coming from the direction of the river.

"You guys stay here in case he comes home," Brooke said sternly to Dave and Leanne who, without question, sat on the veranda and agreed to wait.

Leanne took off her coat and gave it to Brooke. She and Carter walked as close as they could to the water line, heading up the river behind the café. There were old logs and debris banking up along the sides making it hard to get close. Brooke listened; she could still hear the barking. They walked nearly a kilometre along the water's edge.

The sides became small cliff like overhangs of solid rock, you couldn't get to the water's edge, instead walking out onto the ledge you could look down into the water below. The stirred up brown water didn't seem to rise up the rocky edges, in fact, the piles of debris that had accumulated along the sides against the rock seemed like it had moved away from the banks, revealing the muddy bottom. The barking was louder. Brooke squinted through the rain to see Gambit standing down below them on the mud looking at her, barking over and over. He then took off, further up where you could clearly see the years-old debris had shifted. Carter found a spot where the stone walls had a step-down section low enough to jump onto and reached up to help Brooke down after him.

Suddenly the rain stopped. The wind died down; the barking was gone. It was completely still and eerily silent. Brooke felt goosebumps gather on her arms. Carter walked ahead, their feet sinking deep into the mud. Carter stepped up onto a heavy log, pulling Brooke up after him. They looked down over the other side to see Gambit, his little feet pawing desperately at the side of, what looked like, the bow of a small, half buried boat. By the look of it and how damaged it was it would have been buried in the mud and debris for years. Brooke jumped down beside Gambit in front of the boat and tied a rope around his neck, passing the end up to Carter who tugged him up on top of the log beside him.

Brooke stood still. The goosebumps waved up her body from her feet to her hands, the burning in her stomach was so intense she had to kneel down to steady herself.

Even though the boat looked old and damaged, half buried, on the side, she could clearly read the name, written in blue lettering. 'Bonnie Lass'.

Chapter 14

The media frenzy surrounding the discovery of Colin Crawford and his boat was relentless and nationwide. The local and national tv news and newspapers reported the story.

Brooke was shocked to see journalists from 4 major news channels camped in the park across the road under small marquees with cameras set up ready for the live cross to the morning news. There was not a single motel room vacant in town and some were even camping at the caravan park.

A week of foot searches on both sides of the bank, and police divers going over the bottom of the river again reignited a decade long pause in investigations. Back then they declared him dead after 6 months missing and the cause was listed as suspected drowning.

The police recovery and forensic teams came to the conclusion that Colin was indeed on the river that day, he may have struck debris in the water which somehow flipped his boat. They also said the remains of Mr Crawford were found under the boat. He did drown, that's for sure, but they were now led to believe that the small tinny had somehow suctioned itself to the sticky mud on the bottom of the river after capsizing, trapping him inside the hull.

Mayor Gordon and Peter, being in the historical society, spent hours talking to the reporters and writing stories for online blogs. The amount of people wanting to know about Colin's story was amazing. It became a love story; Scottish immigrant meets Aussie lass and settles in a small outback town. It was, in some ways, good for Emery and the local business who would benefit from so many visitors coming to town.

Ollie had managed to convince the news crews that his direct to tent delivery service was vital to their reporting, if they didn't have to leave the tents more than necessary that would be beneficial, and he could do it for them for a small fee.

"Smart boy, that" Dave commented as he came in to get the latest order from Brooke.

"He certainly doesn't waste an opportunity to make extra pocket money, plus it saves one of us doing it, I guess" Brooke couldn't hide her amused smirk as she passed him the box.

Ollie marked it off his list and off he went on his delivery.

Brooke watched the local police paddy wagon pull into the chaos outside, they cleared away lurking reporters and warned them to stay out of the carpark.

"Someone is gonna make a bloody movie about this" James chuckled to Brooke as he ordered his morning coffee. "I can see it now". He rolled his eyes.

"Any news on the break in?" Most people had forgotten about the robbery at Brooke's Place. She still wore a slight black eye and a scar under her brow but was thankful it wasn't worse.

"No leads, no prints, nothing."

Brooke passed the 2 coffees and a box of Dave's choc chip cookies.

"It's on the house, call it a thank you for helping me the other night". James smiled.

"It's my job, Brooke, but I see what you mean, I'm glad you were ok".

Brooke and Carter tried to avoid the media as much as possible, some even pretending to be customers to get information. The local history was updated that day with a decade long mystery solved. This story had been a passed around for 10 years, and changed a little bit every time it was retold, no doubt. Gently the town started to move on, the press started to leave, and the story became history once again but would it really?

Brooke had not seen Colin since she found the Bonnie Lass, maybe he was stuck in spirit here just as much as he was stuck in the hull of the boat. Brooke still had questions with no answers. She thought about the pouch they found in the ceiling, there was something that wasn't right, something still wasn't solved.

Leanne wrapped the remaining cakes to put in the cool room ready to close. Brooke counted the register and placed the money in a bag ready to put in the safe.

"I think you were destined to buy this café. I know it sounds weird, I think you, Brooke, were meant to be here and meant to be a part of this". Leanne looked at Dave for reassurance. Dave sat down and rested his elbows on the table.

"Remember when I told you that souls sometimes don't leave because they have unfinished business, no one wanted this café, no one showed any interest in it for 4 years until, suddenly, you bought it. I'd like to think it's definitely meant to be, you were meant to find him, maybe he had something to do with you seeing that ad that night". Dave's eyes were wide with excitement.

"I'm not sure I believe in that kinda thing". Brooke smiled and walked out the back door to her flat.

Brooke and Carter worked on the roof of the deck together. It felt good to be there, she was happy, every time she looked at him, she felt warmth inside like she had never felt before. Leanne's words the previous day played over and over in her mind. 'You were meant to be here and be a part of this'. She looked across to Carter and the words sank even deeper. She felt a lump building in her throat as she thought about how lucky she was, that this dumb arse pulled over to help her that day. She swallowed hard and the choked, croaky words came out.

"I love you".

Carter turned around sharply, his face looked blank of any expression, he stood there staring at her for what felt like eternity. He took off his gloves one at a time and dropped them on the deck and walked towards her slowly. Her heart beat faster as he stopped in front of her, touching her face one hand on each side of her jaw and kissed her softly.

Chapter 15

Brooke was startled awake by a loud bang on her gate. She had fallen asleep on the couch. Sunday was always a lazy day as it was the only day the café was closed, and Carter had gone on a transport job driving cattle, so she was on her own. She let Gambit out, and he ran in, barking like mad as she stood on the raised garden bed and peered over the top. It was 3 Police officers.

"Hey, Brooke, do you have a minute", Constable McDonald asked as she got down and opened the gate, closing it so Gam wouldn't get out. She directed them in the back door of the café so they could sit down to talk at a table.

"This is Sergeant Townsend from Brisbane, you know Sergeant Williams of course."

Brooke nodded and then shook the other man's hand. "We have come to give you some updates on the investigation surrounding Mr Crawford". Brooke listened intently as the Sergeant opened his folder to read his written notes.

"Mr Crawford, as many locals assumed, had a son who enlisted in the Army, we did submit a claim for that information regarding his whereabouts so he could be informed of the discovery of his father". The Brisbane officer stated. "We did get a bit of intel but a lot of it is classified".

Brooke looked at the paperwork as he spoke.

"Colin and Edith's son was a Warrant Officer, his name is Thomas John Crawford, according to the Army records, served for 30 years with many overseas tours and was highly decorated before he was medically discharged. He never married nor had any children".

Brooke sat back on her chair; her mind alive with theories about his life.

"Thomas Crawford tragically took his own life, Brooke, a few months after he left the Army". James continued on from the other officer. Brooke felt the tears well up in her eyes as he passed an official Army photo across the table to her. To think that Thomas had passed away that way maybe without his parents ever knowing what had become of him was too much for her and she excused herself to grab a tissue from the counter.

She sat back down and looked at the photo. He was quite a handsome man and looked so much like Colin. She realised in that moment that Colin, with no living family, would have no one to claim him.

"I think Colin would want to be buried with his wife, I'd be honoured to accept his ashes if that's possible, we can organise for him to be laid to rest with Edith". Brooke, her voice choking up and her bottom lip quivering, asked to keep the photo of Thomas. The officer from Brisbane agreed.

After the police left, Brooke looked across the carpark to the bench in the park. There sat her Scottish friend. She still held the photo of Thomas in her hand as she walked across and sat down beside him.

"Ahh, wee lass, knew you had it in ya".

Brooke held the photo up. "This is Thomas, your son".

"Aye" he said shortly. "Just as bonnie as his daddy".

She smiled and made a chuff.

"I'll be heading off home now, lass, remember aye, happiness is the key","

Brooke already felt it, the moment she saw him, it was going to be the last time she would see him. Looking back on all they know now, all that they have been through, she was truly grateful to have met him. She smiled and stood up to walk back across the carpark, and when she turned back, he was gone.

Leanne and Kim were overrun with customers for breakfast the next day. Brooke was on the coffee machine nonstop. It was school holidays, so she was grateful to have Ollie helping in the kitchen. The bell ringing on the front door was unusually annoying to her that day, to the point that she intently removed it between breakfast and lunch. She didn't know what was making her feel so cranky but every happy, smiling person that walked through the door only made her fume more. Carter came in for a coffee as the breakfast run ended, she was happy to see him, he was maybe the only little piece of sanity she felt since open. Brooke sent Kim home as Ollie cleared the table closest to her, he didn't put fresh menus on the table. She angrily pulled the drawer out of the counter so hard the entire thing flew out and crashed onto the floor, sending a hundred menus in every direction. Brooke could have cried she was so frustrated, Leanne tried to pick them up, but Brooke insisted on doing it.

She sat down on her knees behind the counter and started to pick them up one at a time. As she picked up the last few, she randomly glanced up to the rectangle hole the drawer had left in the back of the counter. She had been staring into the hole for a few minutes before Carter popped his head over the top to make sure she was ok.

"Happiness is the key". She remembered what Colin said, followed by long gasp. Dave hung his head around the corner of the kitchen door as Brooke ran past him, nearly knocking him over, and flung open the back door with a dreadful crash as out she went. Carter, Leanne, and Ollie stood silently, confused at what was going on. Dave walked to the back door to have Brooke come flying back through it again almost knocking him over again.

"What the hell", he mumbled, following her into the café in disgust. Brooke's face was red, and she was puffing hard as she yelled at Ollie to lock the front door. Ollie didn't argue, he had never moved so fast, turned the closed sign around and locked the door.

"What tha fuck is going on?" Dave looked as confused as everyone else. Brooke finally caught her breath as she pulled Colin's tartan pouch from her pocket.

"I know why the intruders were looking in this drawer". Brooke pulled the old key from the pouch and knelt back down on the floor in front of the hole where the drawer had been. In unison, everyone standing also knelt down with her as she pointed into the drawer. In the back of the drawer was a keyhole, it was big, big enough to fit an old-fashioned key. Brooke reached into the drawer and with a gentle push the big, old key slid into the hole. Her mouth was open as she turned to look at Carter who was kneeling down behind her.

"I'm scared".

 Carter held her hand as she turned the key. It went all the way around once before it latched with a loud click, the silence in the room was deafening, the five of them sat on the floor waiting patiently for something to happen.

"Now what do we do?" Brooke whispered, it was as if, if she made too much noise something would happen. Carter stood up and motioned everyone out of the way, he took hold of the drawer frame and pulled hard. The force of the back of the cupboard moving made him fall back as a puff of dust shot into the air.

They all knelt back down behind the counter. A section of the back had pulled forward and there looked to be a small door. Brooke's nerves were burning in her stomach as Carter reached through the gap, grabbed the side of the door, and pulled it open. It creaked loudly; opening surprisingly easy for something that wouldn't have been opened for years perhaps. The door was roughly a metre square, and it was the entire middle section of the counter. It was dark, Carter felt along the inside of the opening for any sign of a light switch. It wasn't long before he found one, it wasn't a modern switch that went up and down, it was a round dial.

"Here goes nothin'," Carter prayed as he turned the switch. A soft buzzing noise seemed to get louder, the kind of sizzle a light bulb made during a storm, with a few flickers a dull glow lit up the space to reveal a set of stairs going down.

"What do we do now?" Brooke said nervously.

Ollie pushed his way to the front.

"I say we go down, what is the worst that could happen".

Brooke at that point could think of several worst things that could happen. Carter held his hand up blocking his way as he stood up and looked around to make sure no one was around outside.

"I agree, let's go down". Carter took Brooke's hand; he went first, crouching down through the small door led her along behind him. Leanne and Dave were not so keen. Ollie on the other hand was hot on Brooke's heels following her.

There were 6 stairs, Carter stopped on the bottom step, he was able to stand strait now, excitidly gauging the room, the floor had cobble stones like an old street would, and it was the size of a large bathroom. There were light bulbs attached to the walls, a few feet apart, each connected to the next with a black cord attached to the wall around the room.

Brooke stood beside Carter, Ollie beside her. The room was empty except for the back wall. 5 small shelves, about 2 foot long. Each with old, dark glass rum bottles, the round kind with a glass loop for your finger to rest in at the top. There was 20, 4 on each shelf, so dusty you could barely see the shine of the glass. They were sealed with a cork in the top. Carter reached forward and picked up one of the bottles. It was heavy. He pried the cork free, the warmth of the lights in the room amplified the beautiful, rich glow that poured into his hand from the bottle. Happiness is indeed the key. It was Gold.

Chapter 16

Brooke, Carter, Leanne, Dave, and Ollie sat around the centre work bench in the kitchen staring at 20 small rum bottles. They were about 10 centimetres tall and all a dark glass you couldn't see through. No one said a word, they just sat there. The shock was very real. Dave pulled out a set of electric kitchen scales and plugged the cord in under the bench. Carter poured the first bottle into the metal pan on the top of the scale, everyone intently watching the numbers. One after another he did the same to each of the bottles, wrote the number on the front of a menu, making sure he put each bottle's contents back in the one it came from. After the last bottle, Brooke read them out the number. The bottles gold weight ranged from 7 to 40 ounces. Brooke calculated the total was 356 ounces.

"I'm not an expert in gold and what it's worth, but if you go off today's trading prices, I would guess there is over half a million dollars sitting in these jars", Dave suggested.

"I think we need to make a few calls and think about what we need to do". Leanne suggested.

"I wonder how long it's been down there?", Brooke muttered.

Brooke was overwhelmed with the story of Colin Crawford, it just got deeper and deeper the more it went on. Brooke felt scared, having 356 ounces of gold sitting around scared her. They all agreed that they would put the bottles back down in the cellar and Brooke would keep the key in a safe place.

Brooke walked into the police station to talk to James the next morning. He led her into an interview room where she explained what they had found.

"What do I need to do now, is the gold mine?" Brooke gave her phone to James so he could look at the photos she took from the room and the bottles.

"By law, Brooke, you own the property. If you had found the gold while digging and its over 6m underground its classed as mining which will lead to other claims on the gold, but you have found it in a cellar at a property you own, there is no living relatives to Colin, so I would say it's yours".

Brooke was perplexed with the thought of all that gold being hers. She walked out of the station and dawdled down the main street. So many thoughts and feelings flooded her mind. She walked past what was left of the library, suddenly stopping, and holding onto the wire fencing that surrounded it. The burning smell still lingered in the air. She had come to love Emery and the people, the thought of giving back to the community made her happy. She also realised that this was Colin's gold and, in her heart, knew it shouldn't be something she kept for herself. This was Colin's legacy.

Brooke sat on the edge of the creek deck at Carter's hideaway. The sun gave a melted, golden sheen far into the distance, it played on the red soil and green trees, it was such a beautiful place to be. She watched Carter put the last sheet of roofing on the deck. It had become a larger project than first expected but it was theirs together. Carter had built a stone BBQ area from rocks Brooke collected from the creek, and stone steps. Carter also built a wide timber day bed. Brooke had ordered a soft mattress and cushions for it. It really did look beautiful; the deck edge was right above the water so it gave the impression of it floating. For the first time since leaving the city, travelling from town to town, she really felt like she belonged somewhere. Carter crawled across the deck and kissed her.

"Could you see yourself living out here one day?" He asked her.

She looked back across the water and the bush behind it. It was tranquil in its own unique way, it may not be green and lush like a rainforest, but she felt peace every time she was there, the gentle trickle of the water as it ran past, the birds in the trees calling to each other, it was the million stars the sky seemed to have out there compared to the city.

"Yes, I could".

One hundred and fifty people turned out at the cemetery to inter Colin's ashes with Edith. Gordon and Peter led a small service giving a history on Colin to the crowd. A news crew was also there. His ashes were placed in a small dug out section under Edith's headstone. Brooke felt a peculiar sense that the final chapter of Colin Crawford's story was closing. The news of the gold find went through the town quickly. Finding the gold meant that the history of Colin trying his luck back in the day looking for gold wasn't in vain, he did actually hit the mother lode and when he purchased the Blue Bell for Edith, he hid it there and unfortunately died without anyone knowing. This was

Colin's unfinished business, finding his boat but more so finding his gold.

Later that afternoon, some of the locals gathered at Brooke's Place for refreshments. Brooke tapped her fingers on the bell hanging on the back of the door to alert the guests of her need to speak.

"Thank you to everyone who came today and who have shown such an interest in Mr Crawford, we have rewritten history for him twice in the last few months, it makes me proud to have closed the mystery of Colin."

The crowd applauded. "I have had a lot of time to think about The Blue Bell and Colin and Edith. They loved it here, living most of their lives here, it's fitting for Colin's 'Mother Lode' to go back into the town they loved". The applause was louder this time. "After talking to the historical society and the local council, I would like to donate, on behalf of Colin and Edith, 320 ounces of gold to be put forth to re build the Library, Expand the Gold Rush Museum, and repaint the children's ward in a rainbow of beautiful colours". The crowd erupted in cheers and a round of applause that seemed to drift on forever.

Brooke knew that gold wasn't hers and she felt it was wrong to take all of it. She did however keep some. 5 ounces each to Leanne and Dave and 5 ounces would go into a trust account for Ollie which he could use towards university. They were all there when it was found, they were all there from the start when she first came to town, it was right to give them a share.

Chapter 17

Carter pulled his ute into the café carpark. Brooke sat in the passenger seat next to him.

"I wanted to talk to you about the last 16 ounces". Carter turned the engine off and nervously kept hold of the steering wheel. Brooke took a deep breath. "I want to give you the remaining 16 ounces to start building a house at the hideaway. Carter felt a flood of emotions come across his body, he felt his heartbeat quicken, instant sweat across his forehead and a nervous burn in the pit of his stomach.

"I can't, Brooke".

"It's your dream though, I was on the understanding you had me included in that dream, you asked me yourself the other day if I could see myself living out there," Brooke unbuckled the seatbelt and turned towards him, he was still holding onto the steering wheel with both hands.

"I'm sorry, Brooke, I got to go". She looked at him, he was still sitting there, holding the steering wheel, he didn't look at her or say anything. Was he really doing this again?

"Seriously!" she mumbled.

Brooke opened the passenger door and got out. She didn't look back at him, pushed the side gate open and let it slam behind her.

The planning and construction for the new library started within weeks. A team from Templeton Earth Works had started to remove the old library debris with excavators and dump trucks which drew a crowd watching the process. The town had come together, following Brooke's lead, donating their time and services to the project. Brooke continued with the cookie box fundraiser, with the proceeds as originally planned, to go to buying new books.

Emery had become quite busy lately, with tourists coming out to look for gold. Colin's hidden Mother Lode had inspired many prospectors to pick over the already mined out goldfields. The museum was also popular, they had the rum bottles from The Blue Bell on display and a series of photos featuring Colin and Edith.

Brooke sat on the bench where she used to see Colin, it was the anniversary of her mum's death. The sky was clouding over. The change in the weather meant the cooler days would not be as common, they had had so much rain in the past few months, and it would be more humid and hotter now coming into summer days.

Brooke stared into space. So often she had wondered why Colin sat in this exact spot and pondered life. She found a strange comfort in sitting there where he used to. The frustration she felt from Carter was weighing on her mind. He was blowing hot and cold. They had been spending a lot of time out at The Hideaway lately, building the deck roof and creating memories, she thought they were really heading in the right direction. They had been seeing each other for a few months, but it wasn't getting easier. It had been several months since she first arrived at Emery, it certainly felt like years and so much had happened in that time. Sitting there, across the carpark from Brooke's Place, it really hit home. She had everything she could have wanted right across the 20-metre patch of bitumen in front of her, it was the freedom she longed for as a teenager. She needed to shake off the negative energy this day bought every year, she walked back across the carpark, through the gate and past an excited Gambit. She rushed into her bedroom and rummaged under the bed. Gambit was half under the bed with her, his tail wagging.

Brooke puffed hard as she reached for the wooden box that belonged to her mother. She had hidden it there after the robbery in fear that a further break in would have it stolen. It was her mother's box of little things. She walked it out into the lounge room, set it down on the coffee table, and poured herself a glass of red. Her mum collected little random knick-knacks over the years that made her smile or just made her happy, things she loved or that gave her inspiration, it was one of the only keepsakes she took with her from the house after she died. She had added her own little things to the box since she took it. These things were not valuable to others, they were priceless to her, however. These little things, her mother's little things, were more valuable than gold because they were simply hers.

The box had a carved design in the top of flowers, the wood was a dark stain and the small intricate, filigree covered hinges and latch were so old they were starting to come loose from the sides. Brooke opened it slowly. Her mother had collected shells, a piece of driftwood the size of her thumb but it was so smooth to touch it almost felt like suede, cut outs from magazines of places she wanted to go and a packet of seeds. She had added some photos of them both together, a card she wrote to her for her 14th birthday, the one just before she died. The card was worn out from being opened so many times, but the words inside was what she needed today.

"To My beautiful Girl,

Wishing you a magical day for your 14th birthday. You are, and will always be, the first love of my life and I am so proud of you. Never give up on your dreams, never stop shining, for that light is what brightens my day the most. You are so special to me; I love you so much my beautiful girl.

Love Mum.

Brooke ran her fingers over the words. She missed the warmth her mother gave her, the feeling of unconditional love. She opened a small ring box and pulled a sparkling, green stone ring out into her hand and slid it on her pointer finger. Her mum used to wear it everywhere. It was made from a piece of green sea glass she had found when she was travelling in Ireland. Sea glass was something her mum loved to find, she had several pieces in the box, perfectly smooth and different colours. This piece, she said, was special, she said it was lucky, the strong green colour of a 4-leaf clover. 'The luck of the Irish' she used to say when she first found it, she believed it was lucky. In the box, also, was a bottle of perfume, the name had worn off the side and it was half empty but that didn't matter, it was her mum's smell. She held it above her head and sprayed one pump. The smell drifted down like arms wrapping around her, the smell was the warmth, the unconditional love she missed so much. The aching in her heart for that love and connection made her feel lost.

Brooke stood at the bench, poured another glass of red wine as she heard the gate latch. Gambit didn't bark so she knew it must have been Carter. She looked across the loungeroom from the kitchen bench to the front door to see him standing there.

"Can I come in?"

Brooke took a mouthful of her wine and walked back into the lounge, carrying the remains of the bottle, and sat back where the box was.

"Guess so".

Carter opened the door slowly. Walking across to the single armchair, he saw the box and the contents set out on the coffee table. He swallowed hard as he sat down. The silence was thick, dragging on for what felt like forever, before Brooke finally broke the tension.

"I am not in the mood to argue about things anymore," Brooke finished that glass quickly and poured herself another.

"May I?". He asked motioning to the collection on the table. She rested back onto the cushions and nodded. He picked up the largest piece of sea glass and rubbed his fingers across it, then the other smaller pieces. The tinkling sound they made as they touched each other in his hand had a tear fall down her cheek. He saw the open card and perfume bottle. "Are these your mum's?". He barely whispered. She nodded.

"12 years today". Brooke upended her glass, sat forward, and poured the last of the bottle. "Why did you come here Carter?" She put him on the spot. "You couldn't get away from me fast enough this morning".

"I wanted to see you; say I am sorry".

Brooke had enough wine in her for the Dutch courage to kick in and she went straight to the point and didn't hold back.

"I know Rachel was your wife, you feel guilty about her passing, and you still love her, that is perfectly ok", Brooke drank the last of the glass and started to cry. "I can't let you keep me at arm's length anymore, it hurts too much. I told you I loved you, but you want me one minute then push me away the next, whatever this is between us it has to end, before you tell me you can't love me back, because I am not sure if I can handle listening to you tell me that."

Carter sat there for a few minutes playing with the sea glass, leant forward and gently placed them back on the table. He didn't say anything. There was nothing he could say. Because she was right, he reached forward and placed his hand on her knee, she looked up at him, her eyes full of tears. He stood up, slowly turned, and walked back across the room, looked back at her one last time, and walked out the door. Brooke burst into tears.

Chapter 18

It had been three months since he walked out. Not that she was counting. Leanne said he'd told her he was going away working, driving cattle trucks. Brooke assured her, the few times she asked, that she was fine, and everything was ok. Deep down Brooke felt hollow without Carter, the longer he was gone the worse it got.

Brooke placed framed pictures of the newspaper article from the Blue Bell opening on the wall. She also had photos of Colin, Edith, and Thomas beside it. She felt like the room wasn't finished without them.

The café was busy and, with it being 3 weeks till Christmas, she was hosting a lot of family dinners and business Christmas lunches. Erin had come back to Emery to help decorate. She was adamant Brooke couldn't possibly do it on her own. As much as her sister made her brain hurt, she loved her, it was the only family she really had, she just wasn't the best at keeping secrets, if she didn't want dad to know she couldn't tell Erin.

Brooke and Erin had an enormous Christmas tree put up in front of the main set of windows so at night the lights could twinkle a rainbow of colours. They also decorated the front of the café with lights and giant Christmas baubles. They had, Santa's sleigh and a few reindeer on the grass beside the café.

"You ok?" Erin asked watching Brooke mope about. "You have not been yourself at all since I've been back". Brooke shrugged her shoulders.

"I'm fine".

Erin and Brooke worked the café, they were completely booked out for the week leading up to Brooke's Place first-ever team Christmas party and her 28th birthday. All the staff and a few invited customers stayed back on Saturday after the lunch shift for drinks and a bbq. Brooke set up with a table and chairs, and Christmas lights strung across the courtyard. Dave cooked, his wife, Steph, came, Leanne, Ollie, and Peter Archor, Kim, Constable James McDonald, Gordon, Brooke, and Erin. Erin settled into the party well, she seemed to have left her usual stuck-up city chick persona at home this time, soon becoming part of the mismatched family Brooke had around her.

"How is Carter going, Leanne?" Peter asked taking another cold beer from the esky. Brooke sat at the table with James and Erin, and she tried her hardest to listen in without making it obvious.

"He is good, as far as I know, just travelling around taking some time away, hopefully he will be back for Christmas".

Brooke's heart sank a little deeper into her chest. It had been so long since she had seen him, a meeting which didn't end well, she had hoped so much to hear from him, herself, but nothing, not a single text or call in 3 months. Deep down, today, of all days, she hoped to get a happy birthday message or call. Brooke had tried desperately to move on since it became apparent that Carter wasn't coming back. She had recently been on a few dates with James, and they got along well. There wasn't the instant connection, though, no spark but then again, it was very new. She secretly missed Carter, there was just something about Mr Dumb Arse that she couldn't shake off.

"Can I have everyone's attention," Peter announced, tapping a spoon on his beer bottle. Erin came out through the door carrying a cake with candles lit and placed it down in front of Brooke. "Today is Brooke's birthday, as you all know, shall we all sing together". Peter motioned his hands like he was conducting an orchestra. As everyone sang Happy Birthday, she made a wish, and blew out the candles as everyone clapped.

Ollie and Peter left shortly after dessert. Dave and Steph also left as she had early rounds at the doctor's surgery the next morning. Erin and Leanne were 2 bottles of wine deep into an intense game of Poker. James excused himself around 10pm from the group, as he was working the early morning shift and Brooke walked him to his car, he held her hand.

"Thank you for inviting me, I had a good time", James leant in and kissed her goodnight. "Happy Birthday, beautiful", he said wrapping his arms around her. He hopped into his car; Brooke watched him drive away. She stood on the veranda watching the Christmas lights they had set up on the grass near the café. Christmas was always a favourite time of year for her as a child, not so much since her mother died. Brooke always made it a point at Christmas to watch the carols by candlelight on tv, it was something her mother loved to watch, and she felt it was important to try and keep up that tradition. She watched the lights for a while before she re-joined the girls, pouring herself a wine, she sat down hard on the chair with a deep sigh, checking her phone again.

"You been checking that thing all night, you're not holding out for Mr Dumb Arse still are you?" Erin laughed.

Leanne looked across the table at Brooke. "Dumb arse?". She questioned.

"Oh shit," Erin said quickly, knowing she had put her foot in it.

"It was just something silly I called Carter when he pulled over to help me that day, its nothing bad". Brooke looked at her phone again.

"What is going on with the Constable?". Leanne asked her straight up.

Brooke bit her bottom lip trying to swallow the lump building in her throat. "Nothing, it's not serious".

"She is still hung up on your bro". Erin blurted out.

Brooke looked down at her phone, trying hard to not look at them in fear that she would cry. It had been building for months, not talking about him to anyone, hoping he would call. She confided in Erin how she was feeling, which again, she had shown her why you don't tell her secrets. Brooke had so many regrets and mixed feelings. Leanne put her cards down and watched her across the table, fighting back tears.

"Talk to me, Brooke". Leanne pretty much demanded.

"I think I was the one who drove Carter away, I told him I loved him".

Leanne looked surprised but also sympathetic.

"You didn't tell me that bit", Erin protested. "What did the Dumb Arse say?" Erin looked across to Leanne who was giving her a cold stare. "Sorry, what did he say?" Erin took another sip of her wine.

"He didn't say anything back, did he?" Leanne asked.

Brooke didn't have to answer the tears that fell from her eyes said enough.

"If that wasn't all, he asked me if I could see myself living out at the hideaway with him and I said yes, I told him I wanted to give him the last 16 ounces to start the homestead off and he shut me down, then stumbled across me, when I had too much to drink, I pretty much told him I wanted more, I guess him leaving gave me the answer to that".

Leanne felt sad listening, she could see the struggle Brooke was going through. Erin poured more wine in Brooke's glass as she cried. She put her arms around Brooke. Erin wasn't a touchy-feely kind of person, but she could see the comfort she needed.

Four days before Christmas, the new library was nearly done. The community spirit at Emery was infectious as everyone worked together to get the build done. The building was finished, all that was left to do was the working bee and Community Christmas street-party to get the gardens and landscaping finished the next day. Brooke decided she would close the café so she could help.

Before the sun rose on the morning of the working bee, Brooke, Sandra, and a team of volunteers marked out the garden beds with spray paint ready to go. A team of young teenage boys, led by Ollie, unloaded the truck of potted plants and garden supplies. The library was 2 large rectangle-shaped buildings, side by side, that had an undercover central courtyard in the middle, joined by a glass walkway featuring some indigenous sculptures made by amazing local artists, and outdoor rock paintings by the school kids who use the library the most. The front of the building was painted a deep blue, a fitting tribute to Edith and Colin, with wide tiled stairs leading inside. The plan outside was to have raised garden beds with native grasses and bottle brush trees and a blue javelin on each side of the door, also in tribute to the Crawford's, lots of colour and places to sit to read. A collection of large and small boulders collected from the surrounding bush would be dotted through the gardens.

The community turnout was huge, at least 200 people came to help, even if it was just to plant a tree. The council had people setting up the street party which would run after the working bee, also funded from the gold Brooke donated to the town. Market stalls for local producers, BBQ, tables and chairs for catering and a flatbed truck parked for a makeshift stage for the night's entertainment.

People were pushing wheelbarrows of small stones to cover the ground near the sculptures, imitating a creek bed, kids from Emery Creek Primary School helped by planting plants and carrying buckets of bark chips to spread between them. The raised beds were made from recycled railway sleepers provided by the council, the contrast of the rustic wooden sleepers, boulders, and smaller stones was beautiful. Erin was on her hands and knees spreading bark chips throughout the beds, whoever would have thought, after her first visit so long ago, the afraid-to-get-her-hands-dirty city-chick would be doing this. The newspaper sent a photographer to take photos for a special edition.

As the sun started to go down, the outside of the library was finished. Brooke walked along the path, winding through the gardens in the central courtyard. It felt amazing to see it finished. It also hit a deep part of her heart reading the sign proudly displayed at the front entrance. The Colin Crawford Memorial Library. She couldn't explain how proud she felt standing there looking around at the hundreds of people who had helped and were gathered for the street party. There were fairy lights strung across the road and wrapped around the telegraph poles, people sitting at tables eating, people dancing to the local musicians who were taking turns playing. She really felt the feeling of family in the air that night.

She and Erin found a place to sit on some hay bales that dotted the sides of the street just watching the magic.

"I can see why you love it here", Erin smiled, sitting there covered in dirt from the working bee, no time to get showered and changed.

Brooke nodded and put her arm around her sister. "A turnaround from, it's too hot, there are too many flies, blah

blah blah". Brooke laughed as they hugged each other. "I get it, though, I definitely think I have found where I am meant to be".

James, in uniform, came across the road to where they were sitting. He and Paul were doing a walk-through of the crowd just as Gordon Cranston hushed the music and took the microphone. He spoke to the crowd about the day and the amazing community spirit he had seen.

"I am off early in the morning if you want to grab breakfast?" James whispered as she heard Gordon mention her name and the crowd erupted in a roar of clapping. Brooke smiled and waved her hand to the crowd as Gordon thanked her for her contribution to the new library. Brooke looked at James and he knew what she was going to say before she even opened her mouth. "You don't have to say it, I understand".

"I'm sorry, James."

He wasn't angry at her. He knew he wasn't the one she yearned for. James had really grown to like Brooke and wasn't about to let the rejection ruin their friendship. He rubbed her shoulder, a gesture to say goodbye, and walked back across the street to Paul. Erin put her arm around her, Brooke leant her head on her sister's shoulder.

Chapter 19

Brooke drove Erin to the airport early in the morning on Christmas Eve. It was raining heavily. Erin ran down the path carrying her bag, it was a crab-like wobble to get out of the rain. Brooke chuckled, walking along behind her.

"What happened to the girl crawling around the garden getting dirty?" She laughed.

Erin gave her a smug, unimpressed glare. She checked in her bags and the final boarding call came across the speaker.

"Thank you for everything".

Erin hugged her sister tightly. "I'll be back at Easter time. Promise me that you will find that happy spark again". Erin demanded as she squeezed Brooke's hands.

"I promise, I'll give you a call tomorrow". Brooke watched Erin walk out the doors and across the tarmac, again with a weird, bird-like wobble as she ran through the rain to the plane.

Brooke drove her hilux back to town. The rain was heavy, the watery red dirt on the sides of the road sent spatters of mud up the sides of her car. Suddenly the ute started to jolt to the side, the steering wheel jerking back and forth. She managed to pull over onto the shoulder on the side of the road. She jumped out landing in the muddy water and walked around the ute looking for damage, until she found the rear passenger side tyre had blown. The rain had completely soaked her in the short time she had been out. She ran back to the driver's side, leaning in to check her phone, no signal. Brooke slammed the driver's door and let out what probably would have been a loud scream if it wasn't for the rain drowning out the sound. She was completely soaked. Fishing around in the back of the tray she unhitched the toolbox lid. Fumbling around she pulled the jack out and jumped back down off the tray. On her hands and knees in the mud, she positioned the jack under the back axel and hooked the lever onto the side, pumping it up and down to no avail. The jack just sank deeper into the mud the more she pumped it, not lifting the ute up at all. Brooke let out another scream of frustration, kicking her the flat tyre in frustration and stood sobbing in the rain, she didn't know what to do, perhaps, she thought, she should just start walking.

A set of headlights grew brighter and brighter behind her, she turned around to watch a truck pull up behind her ute. It was like déjà vu, a moment in time repeating itself, coming full circle. The rain eased off into a drizzle as she watched a yellow pair of work boots climb one rung at a time down the side of the truck. The man looked unimpressed as he adjusted his baseball cap and walked towards her. He didn't speak to her but knelt down and looked under the back at the jack she was trying to use to change the tyre. He walked back towards his truck, opened the toolbox attached to the trailer, and pulled out a square piece of wooden board. Walking back, he locked eyes with her for a moment and it felt like her heart stopped beating.

Her wet blonde hair suck like glue to her face as the tears flowed evenly down her cheeks with the rain. She folded her arms and watched him unhook the spare from underneath her ute, winding the handle so it lowered to the ground, he slid the board in under the jack to make it stable, pumped the lever and up it went with ease. He changed the tyre, turning the lever on the jack the opposite way so it slowly lowered the ute back down.

He threw the flat into the tray, jumped up on the back and put the jack back in the toolbox before hopping back down, sending a splash of muddy water into the air. He picked up the piece of board and stood in front of her in the rain. He had a beard now; the water droplets ran down and off the end in a continuous drip. She swallowed hard.

"You should probably get a CB radio; phones are useless unless you're in town". Carter adjusted his baseball cap and walked back to the truck, put the board back, and one by one she watched the yellow work boots climb back into the cab.

Brooke, Leanne, and Dave worked a slow Christmas Eve lunch. The café would be closed between Christmas and New Year. Brooke handed each of them a gift to take home.

"Do you have plans for Christmas Day, Brooke?" Dave asked her.

Leanne wiped down the tables with a funny grin on her face, she had been acting strange all afternoon. She put the chairs up ready to mop the floor.

Brooke watched her intrigued. "Yeah, I was just going to stay home actually."

Dave frowned at her. "You are welcome to come and join us if you like, Steph cooks a mean pork roast, best crackle in town".

Brooke smiled and nodded. "Thanks, I'll definitely keep that in mind".

Brooke counted the register, she laid the pile of 10 cent pieces on the bench and started counting before she stopped suddenly, staring at the coin in her hand. Goosebumps prickled up her arms as she realised that in her hand was a Scottish coin, a 1902, Edward the VII, silver shilling. Her hands began to shake as the bell on the door rang, and she looked up to see, one at a time, a pair of yellow work boots step into the room. Carter took off his baseball cap and tucked it under his arm, walked across the room to the counter, and put a box down in front of her. Brooke curled her fingers around the coin and squeezed it tight as she saw it was a CB Radio.

"Is it too late for a coffee?"

Brooke swallowed hard as she saw Leanne across the room with a big smile on her face.

"Black, no sugar". Her voice was croaky as she fought the blurry wave of emotions that wanted to knock her over. She slipped the coin onto the top of the coffee machine in front of her, not able to take her eyes off it. She put the cup down on the bench and pushed the lid gently onto the top, sliding it across the bench to Carter. His fingers touched hers as he reached for the coffee sending a burst of nervous fire through her stomach and goosebumps up her arms. Leanne tapped him on the back with affection then her and Dave turned the sign around on the door as they left, leaving them alone. Brooke fought with everything she had not to cry.

"I know a really top bloke who could install this, if you were willing to give him a chance."

Chapter 20

Brooke lay in bed watching the birds out the window flying in and out of the hollow void in the tree, the babies chirping loudly. It was quiet but noisy at the same time. The sun bounced beams of light off the walls revealing a beautiful morning. She looked beside her to see him lying awake, watching her. He smiled and pulled her closer to him, his strong, muscular arms wrapping around her tightly as he kissed her cheek over and over again.

"Good morning, Mrs Anderson". Brooke breathed him in deeply as he ran his fingers through her hair and down her back. It had been one year today since he walked back into the café. He had spent 3 months driving road trains trying to push through the pain of losing his wife and letting go of the guilt he carried for so many years. He realised while he was on that journey, that he couldn't breathe without Brooke. No one could make him feel as alive as she did. It was like the universe gave him a second chance to stumble across an ignorant city chick needing help on the side of the road, to start over again and turn right instead of left. They tied the knot yesterday in the park across from Brooke's Place, in front of their friends and family. Erin was her bridesmaid, Brooke carried the 1902, Scottish shilling she found the day he walked back into her life. She felt that finding that coin amongst the 10 cent pieces that day was a sign, it spoke to her, like she always used to say, she will know it's right cause 'it will speak to me'.

Carter started building the new homestead at the hideaway, both of their ideas coming together to create a new dream.

Life has a way of finding what's right for you when you need it most. She found the Blue Bell one night, drinking red wine and surfing the internet. The blue Bell Café led her to make amazing friends, it led her to a dumb arse country boy with dimples and a smile that melted her to her core. Together they solved the mystery of Colin and his gold, bought a community together by building the library, and rewrote the history of the town. Most of all, the mismatched group of friends she made became her family. There is far more to family than blood. You make your own family, and she loved each one of them.

Standing on the verandah of the little cabin, looking across at the foundations of their new home, took her breath away. She never imagined that driving into town that day would lead to her standing here, at this moment, having her life feeling so complete. Gambit ran back and forth chasing geckos that scurried around the rocks, he was never going to catch them, they were always smarter, but he kept trying. She remembered what Leanne had said to her that day, she was meant to be there, she was meant to be a part of the story, and what an amazing story it turned out to be.

More books by this author

November
Book 1 in the Calendar Series

The Little Things: Things to Know, Before I go.
A commemorative book of the special little moments of life.